The Dark Between Trees

By Roger D. Brown

"Lost in the forest, I broke off a dark twig and lifted its whisper to my thirsty lips: maybe it was the voice of the rain crying, a cracked bell, or a torn heart.

Something from far off: it seemed deep and secret to me, hidden by the earth, a shout muffled by huge autumns, by the moist half- open darkness of the leaves.

Waking from the dreaming forest there, the hazel---sprig sang under my tongue, its drifting fragrance climbed up through my conscious mind as if suddenly the roots I had left behind cried out to me, the land I had lost with my childhood---and I stopped, wounded by the wandering scent."

--Pablo Neruda

Prologue

Whispering Pines National Park sprawled across the rugged landscape, a hidden realm far from the noise of towns and cities. Here, nature reigned in a dark, untamed beauty. Towering pines stretched skyward, their canopies knitting together like a patchwork ceiling, casting the forest floor in a perpetual twilight. Mist clung to the lower branches, drifting ghost-like between the trunks as evening descended, blurring the lines between tree and shadow.

The air was thick with the scent of charred wood and damp earth. Recent fires had scorched parts of the forest, leaving blackened scars on the ancient pines, their once-verdant needles now brittle and gray. Trails of smoke still lingered in the distance, curling lazily into a sky bruised with the deep hues of twilight. Yet beneath the familiar scents of pine and decay was something more pungent, something unsettling—the faint, coppery odor of blood mingling with the forest's earthy perfume.

Silence ruled the woods, heavy and unnatural, broken only by the soft rustling of leaves stirred by the evening breeze. The trees whispered to each other, their branches brushing together with a low murmur that seemed almost intentional, as though nature itself were holding its breath. Somewhere in the distance, an owl called, its undisturbed. But Caleb was not one to heed warnings, not even those whispered by the wind and the trees.

The forest was quiet now. Too quiet.

In the distance, the last traces of smoke curled lazily into the evening sky, the remnants of the fire that had scorched the edges of the ancient pines. The once-vibrant heart of the Whispering Pines National Park now lay shrouded in shadows, its towering trees bearing the marks of both natural and human destructions. But this fire wasn't the real danger—it was just the distraction.

Beneath the thick underbrush, hidden from the casual eye, something darker stirred.

A lone figure crouched near the edge of a clearing, is gloved hand brushing aside the charred remains of ine needles. He worked silently, quickly, his movements recise as he lifted the animal carcass and examined it ith grim purpose. The body was mutilated, its fur atted with blood, but the wounds weren't from any edator.

They were surgical. Deliberate. Ritualistic.

The figure's breath came out in slow, controlled hales. There was nothing natural about this. He stood, anning the woods, his eyes darting from shadow to adow as if expecting something to emerge from the)om. The wind picked up, whistling softly through the

voice piercing the quiet like an ancient warning.]
beyond that, the forest was still, too still, as thoug
were a creature waiting in ambush.

This land was old—older than the stories tha
been passed down through generations, older th;
settlers who had come and gone. The local Nati
had long believed these woods to be sacred, a p
where the spirits of ancestors dwelled alongside
darker and less forgiving. To them, Whispering
was more than a forest; it was a guardian, a for
own will and purpose, one that did not take kir
trespassers.

Legends of the land told of hunters who v;
without a trace, of travelers who had lost thei
to reemerge days later, changed and hollow-e
something in the forest had stripped them of
It was said that markings—ancient symbols—
carved into the trees by spirits who had once
forest freely and still held power over the liv
these symbols, a jagged spiral, appeared spo
the trees, etched in the bark like a warning.

Caleb Stone knew these legends. He'd
from the locals, from tribal elders who spol
hushed and reverent. They didn't often ven
into the forest, not anymore. Whispering P
secrets, they warned, secrets that were bett

blackened branches, carrying with it an eerie sound—the faintest whisper, as if the forest itself were speaking. But it wasn't words. o, this was something older, something primal—like the low growl of a hidden predator, a sound that seemed to vibrate in the bones and resonate with a hunger that had been dormant for centuries.

A warning.

The man's hand tightened around the handle of his knife. He wasn't afraid—yet—but he wasn't foolish either. He had heard the stories, of course. Everyone in town had. The ancient legends told by the Native tribes who had lived on this land long before the settlers came. Legends of sacred grounds, spirits who guarded the forests, and curses that had never fully died.

But those were just stories. Weren't they?

He shook his head, pushing the thought away. This wasn't the work of some angry spirit. It was people—people who knew exactly what they were doing. He had seen it before, back when he was a sheriff's deputy. Back when everything had gone wrong.

A crack echoed through the trees—far off, but close enough to send a jolt through his body. He turned, eyes narrowing as he scanned the treeline, but there was nothing. Just the whispering of the pines, swaying in the breeze.

This land isn't yours, the whispers seemed to say.

The man exhaled slowly, his heart pounding in his chest. He slipped the knife back into its sheath and began to walk, his footsteps light but determined. He had come to this forest for a reason—to escape, to rebuild, to leave behind the mistakes of his past. But the deeper he ventured into the wilderness, the more it became clear: the forest had its own agenda.

And it wasn't about to let him leave without paying a price.

From the shadows of the trees, a single, jagged symbol carved into the bark caught his eye. A spiral. Sharp at the edges. Old. Familiar.

A shiver ran down his spine. He had seen that mark before.

And he knew—whatever it meant, it wasn't over.

The forest was quiet now. But Caleb Stone knew better than to trust the silence.

Whispering Pines had secrets. And some were better left buried.

Table of Contents

Echoes in the Ashes 1

Hidden Camps 19

The Forest's Warning 39

Beneath the Shadows 54

The Hollow Roots 66

The Hollow Between.......................................78

The Gathering Shadows 91

The Roar of the Pines 108

The Quiet Between Trees..............................127

Where the Trees Remember..........................134

Echoes in the Ashes

The crackle of scorched pine needles under Caleb Stone's boots shattered the oppressive silence that blanketed the forest like an old, heavy quilt. Every step felt as though he was intruding on something sacred—something that had endured the test of time and fire. The acrid smell of smoke hung thick in the air, mingling with the earthy scent of wet ash and burned wood, swirling around him in faint, ghostly wisps. Each tendril of smoke seemed to carry memories of the flames that had devoured the landscape, reducing it to this skeletal ruin. Charred branches jutted out of the ground like broken bones, ancient trees now blackened by the blaze, standing tall but hollow, like sentinels guarding the remnants of a once-thriving sanctuary. They were lifeless, yet somehow, they still seemed to be watching him— waiting.

It was his third patrol of the day, but the weight of the solitude pressed down on him harder than the heat of the sun that barely pierced the dense cover of smoke. The Whispering Pines felt different this time, more oppressive, as though the land itself was whispering secrets too terrible to hear. Caleb paused for a moment, wiping the sweat from his brow, his shirt sticking to his back. He scanned the horizon, looking for any sign of life, but there was none. No animals, no birds, not even the distant rustle of leaves in the wind. Just silence.

Complete and suffocating.

Complete and suffocating, as if the silence itself was a living thing, coiled around the forest, tightening its grip the deeper he went, like a predator waiting to strike.

But that's why he had come here, wasn't it? For the quiet. For the solitude. To escape the relentless noise of his past. The streets of Boston had been too loud, too chaotic, too full of memories he had tried so hard to outrun. The broken relationships, the failed promises, the suffocating guilt—out here, in the untouched wilderness of Idaho, none of that mattered. The towering peaks and endless sky offered him something the city never could: the illusion of freedom.

Caleb's hands tightened around the straps of his backpack as he moved deeper into the charred woods, his breath shallow as the familiar ache of isolation gnawed at him. He had thought he wanted this—the silence, the space, the endless miles of untamed wilderness where no one knew his name or his story. But as the days stretched into weeks, the vastness of it all felt more like a prison than an escape. The fire had only made it worse. What once had been a serene retreat now felt like a graveyard, where the earth itself seemed to shift and breathe, as if something below the surface was stirring, restless and waiting for the right moment to emerge.

He stopped near a fallen tree, its bark peeling away like old skin, revealing the raw, blistered wood underneath. He crouched down, running his fingers over the scorched surface, feeling the heat still trapped within, as if the fire hadn't quite let go. A bitter smile tugged at the corner of his lips. Maybe it never really does, he thought. Maybe the fire just smolders, waiting for the right moment to reignite.

Caleb stood up, his gaze drifting toward the distant ridge where the sun was beginning to set, casting long shadows over the valley. For a brief moment, he let himself imagine what it would be like to leave this place—to abandon the whispering trees and smoke-filled skies. But deep down, he knew the truth. He could never run far enough. Not from the past. Not from himself.

This was his punishment. The endless sky, the silent trees, the weight of memories that pressed in with every breath of smoke-filled air.

His radio crackled on his belt.

"Hey, Stone, you good out there?" Kate Jensen, the park's environmental scientist, spoke in that clipped, professional tone she always used with him—no warmth, no familiarity.

"I'm fine," Caleb answered, his voice low as he knelt by a fallen log. His eyes were fixed on something unusual. His hand hovered above what looked like an animal carcass, but this was no ordinary kill. The flesh had been torn apart with unsettling precision, not by a predator, but by someone—or something—that knew exactly what they were doing.

"Poachers?" Kate's voice buzzed again.

Caleb hesitated, his eyes narrowing at the deliberate cuts. "Not sure. But it's bad."

"Define bad."

Standing, Caleb glanced around. The forest was eerily quiet, too still. "I'll send pictures when I'm back. For now, just stay in the research cabin."

"Yeah, right," Kate replied, sarcasm dripping from every syllable. "Like I'm just going to sit here while you chase shadows. Let me know what you find." She folded her arms, eyes burning with stubborn defiance.

Caleb clipped the radio back to his belt, jaw tight as tension rippled through him. He didn't need another set of eyes here—especially not hers. Kate was relentless, a

4

force of nature when it came to protecting the endangered species in the park, and while he respected her passion, she had no idea what it was like to walk into a scene where the air hummed with something far darker than poaching. He'd seen enough to know the difference. The difference between a crime of desperation and something that felt twisted, almost… deliberate.

The mutilation was meticulous, each cut precise, almost ritualistic. Caleb took a step back, his breath steady but his mind racing, scanning the area for anything that might lead him closer to answers. His eyes drifted over the scattered debris, the broken undergrowth, until something caught his attention. There, carved into the trunk of a nearby tree, just beneath the rough, ashen bark: a symbol. A spiral, jagged at the edges, etched with a disturbing precision into the wood.

His breathe quickened, a chill creeping up his spine. It wasn't the first time he had seen something like this, but the last time had been in a different world—a world where he still wore a badge in a quiet, small town. A world that fell apart in ways he still struggled to understand —a feeling he hadn't been able to shake since Boston.

Caleb's mind flashed back to the alley behind St. Mark's Church, an unforgiving sliver of asphalt barely illuminated by a flickering streetlamp. There, sprawled on the cold ground, he had found the body of a teenage boy, lifeless and discarded like trash. The boy's face was slack, eyes half-open as though frozen in a final, unanswered question. Caleb's hand had trembled as he reached for his badge, the blood-stained metal feeling like a lead weight in his pocket. With his fingers shaking, he'd pressed the radio button, calling for backup in a voice he barely recognized as his own.

Within minutes, others had arrived, but it was the boy's mother who had seared herself into Caleb's memory. She burst onto the scene with a heart-wrenching wail, her raw anguish filling the night air and slicing through Caleb's defenses like a jagged blade. She collapsed beside her son, clutching his hand as if she could will life back into his body. Her cries reverberated off the alley's brick walls, an echo that haunted Caleb in his sleepless nights, in moments he couldn't shake—an echo that had ultimately driven him here, to the edges of civilization, into the shadowed depths of these remote woods.

He had thought that maybe, out here in the wilderness, he could escape the weight of that night. Maybe the silence of the trees would drown out the mother's cries, that haunting reminder of his own helplessness, his own inability to right the world's wrongs. Caleb shook his head, hoping to shake free from the memory, but it clung to him like mist on the forest floor, heavy and cold. The woods around him, dense and shadowed, seemed to absorb his darkness, pulling it into their ancient silence, as though each tree bore witness to the secrets he could never outrun. Here, the forest held his memories, whispered his regrets, and accepted his sins like fallen leaves—buried, but never quite gone.

Suddenly, a rustling sound caught Caleb's attention, sharp and unsettling in the silence. He whipped around, fingers already closing around the hilt of the knife strapped to his side, heart pounding as he scanned the darkened tree line. From the shadows between the towering pines, a figure emerged—tall, broad-shouldered, his presence commanding, even in the dim light. Long, graying hair cascaded past his shoulders, swaying with each slow, deliberate step. It was Chief Tom Standing Bear.

"You found something." His tone was flat, certain, like he already knew the answer. It wasn't a question, but an acknowledgment. He seemed to emerge from the shadows as if the forest itself had willed him into being. His face was etched with the stories of his people, his gaze intense and far-reaching, like he could see beyond the trees and into the very bones of the land.

Caleb exhaled, his hand loosening its grip on the knife, though his muscles stayed taut, ready. With

Standing Bear, it was hard to ever truly relax. The man was an enigma, an ancient figure in modern clothing, and somehow he always seemed to know more than he let on. Caleb had learned long ago that Standing Bear wasn't a man to be surprised by anything.

"Poachers," Caleb said, jerking his chin toward the mutilated carcass. The scene before them was grim, the forest floor splattered with fresh blood, an ugly smear across the serene green landscape. "Maybe more."

Standing Bear moved forward, soundless as a shadow, his boots making no more noise than the falling pine needles. He crouched beside the animal's remains, his eyes dark as he surveyed the deep, jagged cuts. His fingers hovered over the gashes, as if he were reading some message in the brutality. His attention shifted, landing on a symbol carved into the bark of a nearby tree—some crude shape Caleb couldn't decipher, raw and hastily cut. But the sight of it caused something to shift in Standing Bear's face, just barely visible, like a ripple in still water.

"This isn't just poaching," Standing Bear murmured, his voice low and deliberate, as if he were whispering secrets to the forest itself. He brushed the bark with his fingertips, his shoulders squared and his stance grounding him to the earth. When he stood, he rose to his full height, casting a shadow that seemed to blend into the trees, as though he were part of them.

Caleb felt a chill crawl up his spine. He'd seen poaching before—gruesome scenes left by those who took without regard. But this was different. There was an air of calculation to the scene, a deliberate message left in blood.

"A warning," Standing Bear continued, his gaze unreadable. The word hung between them like fog.

Caleb's brow furrowed. "A warning for who?" he asked, his voice a mix of curiosity and unease. Something about the man's tone made him feel as though they were on the edge of something ancient and unforgiving.

Standing Bear met Caleb's eyes, his gaze steady, almost penetrating. "You."

A thread of confusion and irritation tightened Caleb's expression. He gripped the strap of his pack, searching the chief's face for any clue, any sign of what this might mean. "What are you talking about?"

Standing Bear turned his gaze back to the carved symbol, his jaw set with a solemn weight. "This land…" he began, his voice taking on an almost reverent quality. "It's not just dirt and trees. It's sacred. There are forces here that go deeper than anything you've been taught to understand. Things your laws won't protect. Things that won't follow your rules, Ranger Stone."

The words hung in the air, thick and heavy, and Caleb felt a prickle of unease inch up his spine. He'd heard stories from his childhood, tales told around fires late at night about spirits and guardians of the land. Myths, he'd thought back then. Fairy tales. But the conviction in Standing Bear's voice was something different, and he found himself feeling like a trespasser on ground he'd walked his whole life.

Caleb looked from Standing Bear to the mutilated animal, back to the symbol carved into the bark. He forced himself to meet Standing Bear's eyes, though the weight of the man's gaze was almost too much. "So… what? Someone's trying to scare me off?"

"Not someone." Standing Bear's voice was barely more than a whisper. "Something."

Caleb's breath hitched, but he kept his composure, his jaw tightening. "With all due respect, Standing Bear, I'm not scared off by ghost stories."

A flicker of something—disappointment?—crossed Standing Bear's face. "That's what they all say. Until they understand what's at stake. This isn't about you, Caleb. It's about what you represent."

Caleb frowned. "And what do I represent?"

Standing Bear's expression softened, though his gaze never lost its intensity. "The world of men. The laws that turn the sacred into property, the rules that divide land as if it could belong to anyone." He sighed, the weight of his words palpable. "This land belongs to itself, and there are guardians who remember."

Caleb opened his mouth to respond but found he had no words. The conviction in Standing Bear's tone stirred something in him, an instinctual respect for the power of nature—a feeling he'd tried to deny as just superstition. But here, under Standing Bear's unyielding gaze, he felt every bit the intruder.

After a long silence, Standing Bear finally spoke again, softer this time. "Leave this place, Caleb. Take the warning for what it is. Some things are better left in the shadows."

For a moment, the forest fell utterly silent, as though waiting, listening. Caleb felt the weight of the land, of the generations who had walked here long before him, and of those who would walk here long after he was gone.

Caleb bristled, feeling the weight of Standing Bear's words. There was always something cryptic about the chief, a way of speaking that made Caleb feel small in comparison to the vastness of the land. But before he could challenge the chief's ominous warning, Standing Bear turned away, moving deeper into the woods with the same eerie silence, his form dissolving into the trees as if he had never been there.

For a moment, Caleb stood frozen, staring at the spot where the chief had disappeared, the weight of his words hanging heavy in the thick forest air.

Caleb stared after him for a long moment, the words echoing in his head: *This is a warning.*

He took a deep breath, trying to shake off the unease that had settled into his chest. He'd seen his share of strange things, but the chief's cryptic talk about sacred land and warnings wasn't going to scare him off. Still, the carved symbol, the mutilated animal, and the chief's sudden appearance—it all felt like pieces of a puzzle that didn't quite fit together yet.

He turned back toward the carcass, pulling out his phone to snap some pictures for Kate. The last thing he needed was her lecturing him about evidence, but he knew he'd need to show her. Her skepticism was just as sharp as her mind.

As Caleb walked back through the forest, the weight of the symbol and Standing Bear's words sat heavy on his mind. He had come to Whispering Pines to forget the past, to leave behind his mistakes as a sheriff's deputy— the mistake that had cost him everything. But standing there, in the shadows of those ancient pines, he couldn't help but wonder if the forest had its own kind of justice.

The radio crackled again.

"Caleb," Kate's voice crackled through the static, sharp and urgent. "You're going to want to see this."

Caleb exhaled heavily, running a hand over the back of his neck, feeling the weight of exhaustion settle in. He had heard that line too many times today, and each time it seemed to carry worse news. "What now?" His voice was edged with frustration, though he already suspected the answer.

"There's been another... incident," Kate replied, her hesitation making his stomach drop. "A local hunter. Found dead just outside the burial grounds. They're calling it an accident."

Caleb's hand froze mid-motion. "Who's 'they'?"

"Roger Clyde and his crew," Kate said, her voice lowering with unease.

Caleb muttered a curse under his breath. Roger Clyde, the town's mayor, had a reputation for keeping things quiet—especially when it came to anything that could hurt the local economy. Caleb knew the man would bend over backward to keep the tourism dollars and hunting permits rolling in, even if it meant looking the other way when something was clearly off. This was the third death in just two months—too many for anyone to reasonably believe it was all just bad luck.

"Third one, huh?" Caleb muttered, more to himself than to Kate. His gut told him this wasn't an accident, but confronting Clyde and his cronies was always a battle. "I'll be there in ten," he finally said, cutting off the radio with a flick of his wrist. He grabbed his jacket, bracing himself for whatever awaited him at the scene.

As Caleb made his way toward the burial grounds, his mind raced with more questions than answers. The familiar path through the park, once just a stretch of woods, now felt like the edge of something far darker. Standing Bear's cryptic warnings echoed in his mind, intertwining with Kate's unsettling discoveries—the dead animals, the strange patterns in the dirt, and now, a body. It was as if the woods themselves were trying to tell him something, something ancient and angry. He had initially brushed off the signs, chalked it up to local lore or maybe even overzealous poachers, but it was becoming painfully clear—this was more than just poaching. This was something bigger. Something dangerous.

Caleb couldn't shake the feeling that he had walked into something far beyond his understanding when he accepted the job at Whispering Pines. What had seemed like a quiet retreat in nature had turned into a living nightmare, its shadows stretching longer with each discovery. Whatever secrets the place held, they were deep, and someone was clearly willing to kill to keep them buried.

As he neared the burial grounds, he saw the crowd already forming, a low murmur of hushed voices drifting through the trees. The locals huddled together, their faces etched with unease. Even those who had seen death before kept their distance, as if sensing the malevolence that hung in the air. Kate stood apart from the others, arms tightly crossed over her chest, her face pale but resolute, her eyes scanning the scene with the sharpness of someone who had seen too much but wasn't willing to turn away. A few feet away, Roger Clyde puffed out his chest in his usual domineering manner, as if trying to take control of the narrative before it spun too far out of his grasp. His loud voice grated on Caleb's nerves, always a bit too eager to deflect suspicion, but it was Kate's words that stopped him in his tracks.

"Caleb," she called softly as he approached, her voice tight, laced with barely restrained emotion. Her words cut through the stillness of the woods like a thin blade. He stopped, catching her eye, and the look there was enough to tell him everything before she even spoke. "It doesn't add up," she said, a quiet fury simmering beneath her tone. "The way they found him... it looks staged."

Caleb remained silent, his gaze drawn to the body sprawled on the edge of the burial site, half in shadow, half bathed in fading twilight. It was hard to look, yet impossible to look away. The man, one of the local hunters, lay twisted in a way that felt deliberate, his limbs splayed unnaturally, his face frozen in a final grimace that looked more like a mask than the remains of a peaceful end. A rifle rested across his chest, positioned carefully, as though to tell a story. But what story? Caleb's gut clenched, the scene scraping against some primal part of him, something old and wary that sensed danger before it saw it.

The ground was untouched, no signs of a struggle, no evidence of the desperate chaos that usually accompanied such accidents in the wild. The man hadn't simply fallen here, and his death had not been an accident. Caleb knew the signs well enough—he had seen the aftermath of life taken suddenly, the messy, frantic sprawl of bodies that had fought against their fate. But here, there was only an eerie stillness. The rifle, polished and untouched, told its own tale of quiet hands carefully setting the scene, arranging the body like a piece in some grotesque ritual.

This wasn't just a warning—it was a message. His chest tightened with that realization, a deep, cold knot twisting in the pit of his stomach. He could almost feel the eyes of the forest watching him, unseen and unblinking, from the shadows that lingered beyond the trees. He felt as if he were intruding on something, something ancient, something he was never meant to witness. The air around him seemed to thicken, as if even the trees had taken a collective breath, waiting to see what he would do next.

His mind drifted back to his last conversation with Standing Bear, the elder's words ringing in his memory with a strange, unsettling clarity. "This is a warning," Standing Bear had said, his voice grave and low, his eyes dark as the night sky. Caleb hadn't understood it then, had thought it was just one of the old man's cryptic sayings. But now, standing here, looking at the silent warning splayed out before him, it was as if everything suddenly fell into place, like puzzle pieces he hadn't even known were missing.

The forest, these woods he had come to know as a sanctuary, a place of peace and familiarity, now felt changed, foreign—like a stranger wearing the skin of something beloved. He had always felt the woods were alive, but now they seemed sentient, calculating, as if weighing him, deciding if he was to be trusted with the knowledge hidden in their depths.

He crouched down slowly, his fingers grazing the forest floor beside the body, tracing invisible lines between broken twigs, trying to sense what had been taken from this place and what had been left behind. He noticed the hunter's necklace, an old family heirloom, resting beside him as if forgotten, but something told Caleb it was intentional. There were stories about this land, old tales that spoke of spirits who claimed offerings, who whispered in the dead of night, calling the unwary to their doom. The necklace seemed a token, a silent offering made to something beyond his understanding.

Kate moved closer, her face pale in the failing light, her expression one of barely controlled fear and something else—determination, maybe. He saw in her eyes a silent vow, a reflection of the resolve that echoed in his own chest. They couldn't turn back now, couldn't ignore this chilling reminder of what lurked in the shadows of the forest.

"What do you think happened here?" she asked, her voice a tremor of fear and defiance.

Caleb didn't answer right away. Instead, he looked out over the trees, his jaw clenched tight. They'd disturbed something here, something that hadn't yet decided if it would reveal itself or fade back into the shadows. But Caleb knew one thing with gut-wrenching certainty: this was only the beginning.

Hidden Camps

The forest loomed vast and silent as dusk crept over Whispering Pines. Shadows stretched across the forest floor, twisting into strange, unnatural shapes as if the trees themselves were bending toward each other, casting secrets into the growing darkness. Overhead, a bruised sky hung heavy with clouds that seemed to smother the last of the daylight, their weight pressing down on the earth below. A biting chill threaded through the dense thicket, tinged with the scent of damp soil and the lingering memory of smoke from a distant, smoldering fire.

The wind was a faint whisper, threading through the branches in broken fragments that might almost have sounded like words to anyone listening closely enough. But here, in the heart of the wilderness, there were no familiar sounds of life—no birds calling their last notes of the day, no rustling of creatures settling in for the night. Instead, an oppressive stillness blanketed the trees, a silence so absolute that each crackle of a fallen leaf or snap of a twig seemed to echo louder than it should.

Somewhere deep in the forest, hidden from view, the presence of an ancient altar weighed on the landscape, a relic of another time and purpose. It was as if the land remembered, as if it was holding its breath, watching and waiting for those who might dare to break its quiet solitude. The air was charged, carrying an energy that prickled the skin, foreboding and cold, pressing like a warning against anyone who dared to walk its trails.

Amidst this living silence, Caleb trudged onward, his steps heavy with both physical and emotional weight. The world around him seemed to darken further with each step, shadows deepening as if they too held their secrets tight. The familiar path to the research cabin felt strange and unfamiliar, transformed by the events of the day into something darker, something alien.

The chill of dusk had settled over Whispering Pines as Caleb trudged back toward the research cabin, the weight of the day's discoveries bearing down on his shoulders like a heavy yoke. His breaths were shallow, labored, as if the air itself was thickening, filled with the heaviness of the woods that now seemed to pulse with an energy he couldn't quite place. His mind was still on the hunter's body, a grisly puzzle that refused to fit neatly into any explanation. The signs were all there—deliberate, staged, ritualistic. It felt as if the woods were unraveling before him, revealing a darkness he hadn't been prepared for. And Kate's words echoed in his head: *It looks staged.*

He clenched his jaw, trying to shake the image from his mind, but it clung to him like a shadow. The distant chatter of the gathered crowd—park rangers, volunteers, and those damn reporters—faded as Caleb entered the thickening forest. His boots crunched over the fallen pine needles, the sound eerily similar to the crackle of scorched earth earlier that day, and each step seemed to carry the weight of something more than just exhaustion. The forest seemed quieter than before, the oppressive stillness wrapping around him like a suffocating shroud. The trees, usually familiar sentinels standing tall, felt foreboding now, casting long, twisted shadows in the fading light. The further he went, the more the unease settled into his bones.

He hadn't wanted to drag Kate into this, but there was no avoiding it now. She'd seen too much, sensed too much. The urgency in her voice when she'd called over the radio had been enough to confirm that she wasn't going to let this go. She'd never been one to sit back, and that fire, as much as it grated on his nerves at times, was something he respected about her. Kate was relentless, driven, and fiercely protective of the park and its inhabitants—both human and otherwise. But her determination could be a double-edged sword, and Caleb could already feel the impending clash between them brewing as he made his way toward the cabin. There was something in the way she had looked at him before they parted, a flicker of something more than just professional concern.

The cabin came into view through the trees, dimly lit, its modest silhouette blending into the surrounding woods. A gust of wind swept through the clearing, sending a flurry of pine needles swirling across the path, and for a moment, Caleb hesitated. He could see Kate's shadow moving inside, backlit by the faint glow of a desk lamp. She was pacing, her usual calm replaced by the restless energy he had come to recognize as a sign she was deep in thought—likely already forming theories, asking questions he wasn't ready to answer.

Caleb took a deep breath, steeling himself for what was bound to be an unpleasant conversation. He wasn't in the mood for another debate, especially after the day's events, but there was no avoiding it now. His hand hovered over the cabin door for a moment, feeling the coolness of the wood beneath his fingers. Inside, Kate would be waiting, ready to pick apart the mystery piece by piece until nothing was left but raw truth. And after what they'd seen today, Caleb wasn't sure if he was ready to face that truth just yet.

As he opened the door, Kate was already standing by the window, her arms crossed tightly over her chest, her eyes sharp and focused. The tension in the room was palpable. She didn't turn to greet him, her gaze fixed on something far beyond the glass, as if searching for answers in the twilight sky.

"Did you get the pictures?" Caleb asked, his voice gravelly with fatigue. His body ached from days of restless nights, and the weight of the situation hung heavily on his shoulders.

Kate finally looked at him, her face drawn but resolute, eyes filled with a mix of anger and sorrow. "I got them," she said, her voice steady, though the slightest tremor betrayed her unease. She moved toward the desk where her laptop sat open, the screen flickering with the gruesome images Caleb had sent. "This isn't just poaching, Caleb. We both know that."

He let out a breath, stepping closer to the desk. His eyes flicked over the images once again, each one a brutal reminder of the scene he had witnessed firsthand. The sight was no less disturbing on a screen. "I never said it was," he replied, his tone low and grim. He rubbed his temples, trying to push away the exhaustion clouding his thoughts. "But this... this is something else."

Kate's lips pressed into a thin line, her arms wrapping around herself a little tighter. She leaned against the desk, her knuckles turning white as she gripped the edge. "Standing Bear thinks it's a warning. A spiritual one."

Caleb's head snapped up, his brow furrowing in confusion. "A warning? What does that even mean, Kate? Do you believe him?" His voice was skeptical, though not dismissive. He trusted Standing Bear, but this—this was beyond anything he could rationalize.

"I don't know what to believe," Kate admitted, her tone softening, but no less determined. She turned to face him fully, her eyes searching his. "But I do know that the poaching, the mutilations, the symbols... they all started after the government announced the new logging contracts. It's not a coincidence."

Caleb exhaled heavily, rubbing the back of his neck, the tension in his muscles refusing to ease. "Roger Clyde is behind those contracts," he muttered darkly. "He's pushing harder than anyone, and he's got the whole town council in his pocket."

Kate's expression darkened at the mention of the mayor's name, her eyes narrowing with barely concealed contempt. "Clyde only cares about money," she said, her voice dripping with disgust. "He doesn't give a damn about the park or the people who live here. If it means more hunting permits and logging rights, he'd sell this entire forest without a second thought."

Caleb nodded, his gaze hardening. "Yeah, and we're the only ones standing in his way. You, me, and Standing Bear. That's not a lot of backup."

Kate's jaw clenched. "No, it's not," she agreed, her tone grim. "But it's enough if we keep pushing. We can't let this slide, Caleb. We can't let Clyde and his goons get away with this."

"I'm not letting it slide," Caleb shot back, his voice firm. "But we need more than just us. We need proof. We need something that'll hold up in court or in front of the media. Otherwise, Clyde will bury this, and us along with it."

Kate's eyes flashed with determination. "Then we'll get the proof. We'll talk to the locals, to the rangers, to anyone who's seen something. Someone knows more than they're saying. And if they won't talk, we'll find another way."

Caleb ran a hand through his hair, frustration clear on his face. "You make it sound easy. But you know what Clyde's capable of, Kate. He's not going to play fair. He never does."

Her gaze softened slightly, but the resolve in her voice didn't waver. "I know it won't be easy. I'm not naive. But what choice do we have, Caleb? If we do nothing, more animals will die, more land will be lost, and this place... this place we love will be gone forever."

Caleb looked at her, his heart heavy with the weight of her words. She was right, of course. She always was. He sighed, stepping closer to her, placing a hand gently on her shoulder. "We'll stop him, Kate. We'll find a way."

She nodded, her eyes softening for the first time since he'd walked in. "We have to," she whispered. "For Standing Bear. For the people here. For everything this place stands for."

Caleb's grip tightened ever so slightly, a silent promise passing between them. They were in this together, no matter how dark the path ahead might become.

Caleb couldn't argue with that. Clyde had made it clear from day one that he saw the park as a resource to be exploited, not protected. But the more Caleb thought about it, the more he realized that this went beyond Clyde's greed. There was something else at play, something darker, and Standing Bear seemed to know more than he was letting on.

"Standing Bear mentioned something about sacred land," Caleb said, his voice low, breaking the silence that had been hanging between them. "He said this was bigger than poaching. Something about forces that don't follow our laws."

Kate raised an eyebrow, her expression one of curiosity mixed with skepticism. "Forces that don't follow our laws? What's that supposed to mean? Are we talking about people, animals, or something else entirely?"

Caleb exhaled, his frustration evident. "I wish I knew. Standing Bear wasn't exactly eager to clarify, but it sounded like he was hinting at something supernatural. Or at least, something beyond the normal scope of what we deal with."

Kate crossed her arms, leaning back slightly as she processed what Caleb was saying. "Supernatural? You really think that's what he meant? Or could it be more symbolic, like how some tribes view the land itself as a living entity?"

"I don't know," Caleb admitted, shaking his head. "But whatever's happening here, it's not just about animals or logging permits. It feels... deliberate. Like someone—or something—is trying to send a message."

Kate's eyes narrowed, her mind clearly racing. "If Standing Bear's tribe believes the land is sacred, then they might see any encroachment—whether it's logging or poaching—as a violation. That much I can understand.

It wouldn't be the first time something like this has happened. But the mutilations..."

She trailed off, shaking her head as if she couldn't quite wrap her mind around it. "They don't fit. They're too brutal, too calculated. It's like someone is making a point, but I don't see how it connects to the land being sacred."

Caleb leaned against the desk, crossing his arms as he tried to piece it all together. "So, what do we do? Go to Standing Bear, ask him to explain his cryptic warnings? Or do we confront Clyde and see if he'll admit to being behind all of this?"

Kate's jaw tightened, her frustration mirroring his. "Clyde won't admit to anything, Caleb. He's too clever for that, and he knows how to cover his tracks. And Standing Bear? He won't talk unless he's ready, and even then, he'll probably keep half of it to himself."

Caleb nodded, his mind working through the same dilemma. "We're stuck between two sides, both with something to hide. And we don't have enough information to trust either of them fully."

Kate sighed, running a hand through her hair. "Great. Just what we need—a mystery wrapped in another mystery. So, what's our next move? We can't sit around waiting for someone to hand us the answers."

Before Caleb could respond, the radio on his belt crackled to life again, making both of them jump slightly. The voice that followed was calm, yet carried an unmistakable weight.

"Chief Standing Bear here," the voice said. "Caleb, you need to come to the ridge. We've found something. Bring Kate."

Caleb exchanged a glance with Kate, the unease between them palpable. "Well," he said, grabbing his jacket, "looks like we're getting answers tonight. One way or another."

Kate hesitated for a moment, then followed suit, pulling on her own jacket. "Let's hope the answers don't bring even more questions," she muttered, glancing at Caleb as they made their way toward the door. "Because I have a feeling this is just the tip of the iceberg."

Caleb nodded grimly, his hand resting on the door handle. "Yeah. Something tells me we're not going to like what we find up there."

With that, they stepped outside, the cool night air hitting their faces as they headed toward their vehicle, the weight of whatever awaited them on the ridge hanging over them like a storm cloud ready to break.

The two of them moved quickly through the darkened forest, their flashlights cutting narrow beams through the smoky haze that still lingered. Each step felt labored, as though the weight of the air itself was pressing down on them. The ridge wasn't far, but the steep ascent made it feel longer, every step filled with a growing tension. Caleb's breathing became shallow, and he couldn't shake the feeling that they were walking into something far bigger than either of them had anticipated.

"Are you sure about this, Kate?" Caleb asked, his voice barely above a whisper. He could hear the crunch of her boots just behind him.

"Not even a little," she muttered, her flashlight sweeping through the trees. "But we're here now."

When they finally reached the ridge, Standing Bear was already there, his tall figure silhouetted against the darkening sky. His presence was imposing, like a sentinel that had been there long before the world around them had darkened. He stood beside a group of his tribe's elders, their solemn expressions matching the heavy air that hung around them. The scene felt like it was plucked from an ancient story, one where the earth and sky met for a reckoning.

As the darkness thickened, Caleb found himself rooted to the spot, mesmerized by the eerie aura emanating from the altar. His eyes traced the crude symbols, each jagged spiral and line exuding an unsettling sense of purpose. The wind had died, leaving only the faint echo of their breathing and the muted rustle of unseen creatures lurking just out of sight. He glanced at Kate, her face drawn and pale, her gaze fixated on the altar as if hypnotized.

Standing Bear's voice cut through the silence, low and reverent. "This is not just a place—it's a threshold. Our people have known it by many names, but one thing has always been clear: to cross it uninvited is to invite wrath." His gaze shifted to Caleb, his eyes holding the weight of generations. "You've come to understand that the forest is more than roots and branches. But this…" He gestured toward the altar, his voice trailing off, as if the very words carried a curse. "This is a reminder. A warning."

Caleb's fingers tightened around his flashlight, the chill in his hand spreading up his arm. "A warning for what?"

Standing Bear's eyes didn't waver. "To remember what we've forgotten. That there are things here older than our memories, older than us."

Kate's hand went to her chest, as if she could physically hold down the fear rising within her. "This… doesn't feel like any place I've seen before," she murmured, barely more than a whisper. Her voice cracked with an edge of awe mingled with dread. "I've hiked through these woods my whole life, but I've never felt anything like this."

"Because you haven't ventured this far into their domain," Standing Bear replied, his voice carrying the cadence of an ancient chant. "Few have. Those who have rarely come back unchanged."

A shiver ran down Caleb's spine. "You're saying people have… come here before?"

Standing Bear nodded slowly. "Long ago. But they did not heed the warnings. The forest—this place—claims what it must."

The words hung in the cold night air, settling like a shroud over the three of them. Caleb's instincts screamed at him to leave, to turn back the way they had come, but something held him in place. It was as if an invisible hand had reached out from the darkness, rooting him to the ground, pulling him closer to the altar.

Kate's voice broke the silence, hoarse and trembling. "Caleb, what if he's right? What if we've woken something… something that was better left alone?"

A strange, low hum rose from the forest, a sound that made the hairs on the back of Caleb's neck stand up. It was subtle at first, an almost imperceptible vibration in the air, but it grew, spreading through the trees like a living pulse. The sound seemed to come from everywhere at once, a primal chant that resonated deep within his bones.

Standing Bear's eyes narrowed, and he muttered a few words in his native language, his tone grave and focused. Caleb recognized the look—one of ancient knowledge meeting present-day terror.

The hum intensified, becoming a low growl that rumbled through the earth beneath them. Caleb felt his pulse quicken, mirroring the rhythm of the strange sound. He glanced at Kate, her face pale, her breathing shallow as her eyes darted between him and Standing Bear.

Suddenly, there was a snap—a branch breaking in the darkness. All three of them turned, flashlights piercing the trees, but the beam seemed swallowed by the shadows, as though the forest had learned to resist the light itself.

"Did you see that?" Kate's voice was barely a whisper, but the terror in it was unmistakable.

Standing Bear shook his head, his expression darkening. "The forest knows we are here. It's testing us. We must respect it, or it will force us to."

"But how?" Caleb asked, voice tight. "What do we do?"

Standing Bear moved closer to the altar, his movements slow, deliberate. He raised his hands, his eyes closed, murmuring words that sounded ancient, a language older than time itself. His voice was calm, but Caleb could sense the tension underlying every syllable, as though even speaking in that language risked disturbing forces far beyond their control.

Caleb's flashlight flickered, the beam struggling as if it were fighting against the very darkness around them. His breath quickened, and a bead of sweat traced a cold path down his back.

And then, suddenly, all sound ceased. The forest went silent, the hum, the growl, even the subtle rustling all vanishing in an instant, leaving only the profound, crushing silence of the night. It was as if they were the last beings in the world, standing on the edge of a reality where time and nature blurred together into something unfamiliar and menacing.

Standing Bear lowered his hands, his eyes now darker than ever. "We've been granted a moment," he said, his voice trembling slightly. "A chance to leave, to step back from the edge. But it won't come again."

Kate reached out, clutching Caleb's arm tightly. Her fingers were cold, and he felt the desperation in her grip. "Caleb, let's go. This is… this is beyond us."

Caleb looked at her, then at Standing Bear, and finally back at the altar. His instincts screamed to retreat, to pull Kate away from this place and never return. But something deep within him, a primal urge, kept him rooted, a part of him refusing to turn his back on the ancient mystery unraveling before him.

"We should go," Standing Bear warned, his voice firm. "Before it's too late."

But Caleb took a deep breath, his gaze steady as he turned to face the altar. He raised his flashlight again, illuminating the symbols one last time. He felt the weight of the forest pressing in on him, the sense of countless eyes watching from the darkness.

And then, just as he was about to turn away, a single word appeared in his mind, unbidden yet certain—a name, or perhaps a warning. It was a word he did not recognize, something older than any language he knew, a sound that felt like it belonged to the earth itself.

"Caleb!" Kate's voice cut through his trance, snapping him back to the present. She was pulling at his arm, her eyes wide with fear.

He nodded slowly, turning to follow her, but as they left the altar behind, he couldn't shake the feeling that something ancient and unseen was watching, marking him. The forest had spoken, and he knew, deep down, that they hadn't truly escaped.

As they walked back through the trees, every sound seemed amplified—the crack of a branch, the rustle of leaves, each noise echoing like a heartbeat through the darkened woods. The forest seemed alive, aware, and Caleb felt its presence settling into his bones, lingering long after they had left the altar behind.

And somewhere in the darkness, the ancient hum began again, a whisper that faded into the night, a reminder that the forest never forgets.

He forced himself to take a step back, but the forest felt like it was pulling him in, binding him in place. Every instinct screamed that they were no longer alone. Shadows moved at the edges of his vision, shifting in ways that defied reason, shapes half-glimpsed in the dim light. Somewhere above, a raven's harsh call shattered the quiet, its echo resonating like a warning.

Kate turned to Caleb, her eyes wide, searching his face for answers. "What do we do?" she whispered, barely holding back the tremor in her voice. "We can't just leave this…whatever it is."

Caleb swallowed, his throat dry as dust. "We don't have a choice," he replied, his voice steady but uncertain. "We need more information. We can't fight something we don't understand." Even as he spoke, he felt the weight of the words, an instinctive sense that maybe he didn't want to understand whatever lurked within the trees.

Standing Bear's gaze never wavered, his eyes dark and resolute, locked onto Caleb's with a calm intensity. "You don't fight this," he said quietly, each word like the strike of a drum. "You either respect it—or it consumes you."

A hush fell, so complete that Caleb could hear his own heartbeat thudding in his ears. The forest leaned in, closer than before, the trees bowing and shifting in strange, unnatural sync. The rustling grew louder, an unseen pulse within the wood that seemed to throb with a life of its own. Caleb glanced down, watching in horror as the roots below his feet seemed to writhe, curling and unfurling, threading through the soil as if to encircle them.

Kate grabbed his arm, her fingers digging into his jacket sleeve. "Caleb…" she whispered, her breath warm against the chill. "What…what is happening?"

But there were no answers. Caleb felt the weight of a thousand unspoken words in the stillness, words that had been buried in the forest's dark soil, waiting to be heard, waiting to be reckoned with. He met Standing Bear's gaze again, feeling the ancient knowledge simmering behind his calm exterior.

"We've woken it," Standing Bear murmured, barely more than a whisper. "The forest remembers. And now, it's watching."

The hair on the back of Caleb's neck prickled as a gust of wind whipped through the clearing, carrying with it the scent of damp earth and decay, of roots and rot. He felt an urge to flee, every fiber of his being screaming for him to run. But he knew instinctively that there was no escape—that they were already in too deep.

For a moment, he considered speaking, saying something to break the terrible, fragile silence. But words felt empty, meaningless in the face of such vastness. The forest had become something primal, something that transcended logic or language. And whatever lay beneath its surface, waiting in the shadows, was beyond anything they could have prepared for.

Standing Bear took a step back, his eyes never leaving Caleb's. "This land has its own justice," he said, his voice carrying an edge of finality. "And it will be carried out, whether we stand here or turn away."

As he spoke, a branch cracked somewhere to their left, loud and final. It echoed through the trees like a shot, and Caleb felt a chill seize him, his pulse freezing in his veins. The forest had spoken, and it felt like a warning—a final chance to respect its power... or be swallowed by it.

The Forest's Warning

The forest lay heavy under a sky bruised by twilight, where the last wisps of daylight surrendered to the grip of night. Whispering Pines seemed almost sentient, a mass of trees that swayed with a collective consciousness, their dark branches knitting together to obscure the fading glow above. The air held a damp chill, laden with the rich, earthy scent of moss and decaying leaves, mingled with an unsettling sharpness that hinted at secrets buried in soil older than memory.

A thick fog had settled low to the ground, threading between tree trunks like silent phantoms, shifting as if alive, concealing the uneven terrain beneath. Shadows moved with purpose, playing tricks on the eyes, making even the smallest gust of wind seem like a hidden presence slipping between the trees. The only sounds were the occasional drip of condensed moisture falling from branches and the distant rustle of something unseen moving deeper in the woods, its pace slow and deliberate.

The burial grounds lay just beyond a natural clearing, an ancient circle of stones half-swallowed by moss and creeping ivy. They stood like solemn sentries in the fog, bearing the weight of history as much as the fog itself. It was as if the land held its breath here, each rock and root imbued with a timeless energy that watched and waited. The pines loomed like silent witnesses, their roots tangled in the past, guarding secrets that Caleb could feel but not yet understand.

Caleb Stone gripped the edge of his truck's steering wheel with white-knuckled intensity, the leather creaking beneath his fingers. The narrow dirt road snaked through Whispering Pines like a forgotten vein, its rugged path illuminated only by the faint glow of his dimming headlights. Heavy mist rolled off the looming mountains, clinging to the trees like a shroud. The deeper he drove into the forest, the more the night seemed to close in on him. The pines, once stately, now twisted into dark, towering sentinels, their shadowed forms reaching out like skeletal fingers. It was as if the forest itself was alive, its breath a low whisper in the wind. Caleb felt the hair on his arms prickling beneath his jacket. He wasn't easily rattled, but there was something about this place that seemed... off. Like it was holding its breath, waiting.

The oppressive silence was broken by the crackle of his radio, a burst of static that startled him enough to make his grip slip. "Caleb, you there?" Kate Jensen's voice cut through, edged with a mix of concern and urgency that Caleb had only heard a few times before. Her voice was steady, but there was a faint tremor there—a sound that would be easy to miss unless you knew her as well as he did. And Caleb did. He knew how she looked when she was trying to keep her nerves in check, the way she bit the inside of her lip when things felt wrong.

He reached for the radio, hesitating for just a second before pressing the button. "Yeah, I'm here," he replied, keeping his voice even, though his pulse had quickened. "Just a couple of turns away from the ridge. What's going on? You sound spooked."

"I'm already here," she answered, and the faint crackle of wind through the radio made her voice sound far away, almost ghostly. "Standing Bear's with me, along with two of his elders. Caleb, it's... it's not just about poaching anymore. There's something else. Something bigger."

Caleb's jaw clenched as he took a sharp curve, gravel grinding beneath the tires like teeth on bone. He had known from the moment he'd found that first carcass— its body splayed out like some macabre offering—that this wasn't just another wildlife management case. The positioning had been too deliberate, the wounds too precise, as though someone—or something—had wanted to send a message. But hearing Kate say it out loud made his chest tighten, the reality sinking in like a cold weight.

A few minutes later, he pulled into the clearing. The truck's engine grumbled to a stop, its headlights casting long, wavering beams that barely held back the darkness. He killed the lights, plunging the world back into the dim haze of dusk and fog. Ahead, the burial grounds emerged, a somber circle of ancient stones and earth that seemed to bear the weight of countless lifetimes. The glow of flashlights bobbed through the mist, and Caleb spotted Kate, Standing Bear, and the elders, their figures casting distorted shadows across the ground. Their faces were pale in the light, their expressions a grim blend of fear and something else—something ancient and knowing.

Caleb stepped out of the truck, the chill night air wrapping around him like a damp sheet. He moved towards the group, his boots crunching over dried leaves and brittle twigs. "What did you find?" His voice was gruffer than intended, carrying the strain of too many sleepless nights and unanswered questions.

Standing Bear turned to face him, his dark eyes reflecting the flashlight's beam. The man's presence was like the mountain itself—steady, unwavering. "Another symbol," he said, his voice a low rumble that seemed to resonate through the very ground they stood on. He gestured toward a nearby tree. "There." The spiraling mark gouged into the bark was jagged and raw, the edges still fresh and seeping sap like the tree was bleeding. It mirrored the one Caleb had found days ago during his patrol, another dark omen etched into the forest's skin.

Caleb's gaze lingered on the symbol, a knot forming in his gut. "There's more, isn't there?" His tone was flat, but his eyes were searching, shifting from Kate to Standing Bear.

"Come see for yourself," Standing Bear said, his expression unreadable as he turned and led the way. The chief's silence was weightier than words, like he knew there were things best left unspoken.

Caleb followed, the elders trailing close behind with grim faces. They made their way down a narrow path lined with stones, the air growing colder and heavier with each step. As they approached a shallow depression in the earth, Caleb's heart sank. The stench hit him first—coppery and sour, a scent he had come to associate with death. Lying within the pit was another animal, its body twisted and broken, limbs splayed at unnatural angles. Blood matted its fur and seeped into the soil. The mutilations were methodical, deliberate, almost surgical. There was a sick kind of artistry to it.

Kate stepped beside him, her arms wrapped tightly around her midsection, as if bracing against the sight.

"This isn't just poaching, Caleb," she murmured, her voice barely above a whisper. "It's ritualistic. Like… someone's trying to call something here."

He glanced at her, noting the way she kept her eyes on the animal. "Call what, exactly?" His tone was sharp, frustration edging in. He wasn't in the mood for vague warnings and folklore.

Standing Bear knelt beside the carcass, his movements slow and reverent. "It is not our way," he said, almost to himself. "But there are those who have forgotten the old ways, who seek to stir forces best left undisturbed." He stood, turning to face Caleb, his gaze unflinching. "You think this is just men with guns, taking what they shouldn't?" His voice dropped lower, more intense. "No. This is something older, something rooted in the land itself. The lines between the living and the spirit world… they blur when the land is disrespected."

Caleb stared at the chief, his jaw tightening. "You mean the poachers," he said, though there was a question in his tone. "You're saying they're trying to… what, summon something? Are you serious?"

Standing Bear's gaze did not waver. "Not summon, perhaps. Awaken," he corrected quietly. "There are spirits in this place that have slept for centuries, bound by old rites and ancient agreements. But there are some who think they can break those bonds, stir the earth and sky as they please. These symbols… these sacrifices... they are a warning. Or a calling."

The words hung in the air, their weight pressing down on Caleb's chest. For a moment, he glanced back at the trees, half expecting to see something moving between the trunks, some shadow with too much shape. He forced himself to exhale, shaking off the chill that had settled deep in his bones.

"Well, then," he said, his voice rougher than he intended, "I guess we'd better figure out who the hell thinks they can play with forces like that. And make damn sure they don't get the chance to try again." He looked to Kate, then Standing Bear, and finally to the elders. "Whatever this is… we're going to stop it." His tone left no room for doubt, though inside, a tiny flicker of uncertainty remained, gnawing at him like the dark edges of the forest itself.

Caleb was about to ask for clarification when a rustling sound echoed through the towering pines, the whisper of movement slicing through the quiet. The elders tensed, eyes narrowing and shoulders stiffening in unison, as though responding to a shared and ancient understanding. Their glances spoke of unspoken knowledge, secrets traded between generations. Instinctively, Caleb's hand moved to the flashlight clipped to his belt. He drew it out in one swift motion, directing the beam into the dense wall of trees where the noise had come from.

The light sliced through the darkness, illuminating gnarled trunks and weaving shadows that danced along the underbrush. But there was nothing—no sign of life, only the blackness that seemed to pulse just beyond the flashlight's reach. A chill laced the air, threading through the leaves that clung stubbornly to the trees. In the depths of the woods, the stillness felt unnatural, a silence too heavy to be merely the absence of sound.

Beside him, Kate shifted, her boot scuffing against the damp forest floor. "Maybe we should head back," she murmured, her voice lower now, almost reluctant to break the tension hanging in the air like mist. "It's getting late, and we're not exactly equipped for... whatever this is." She cast a wary glance over her shoulder, her unease palpable in the fading light.

Caleb glanced at her, then back at Standing Bear. The old chief's face was a mask of contemplation, his gaze fixed on the darkness as if it held answers only he could see. "Do you think it's connected to the logging contracts?" Caleb asked, his voice edged with a frustration that had been growing in his chest ever since he'd arrived. "Or are we just chasing shadows here?"

Standing Bear turned to face him fully, and in the dim light, the weight of his stare was almost tangible, as though he was looking through Caleb rather than at him. "The logging," he said slowly, "is a catalyst, but not the cause." His voice seemed to vibrate with an old resonance, a deep current of history that rippled through his words. "These lands are older than any treaty, any government decree. Those who seek to profit from them without understanding the consequences awaken things they cannot control. The spirits of this place are not bound by our rules, Caleb," Standing Bear continued, his eyes narrowing. "They were here long before us, and they have no mercy for those who tread where they should not."

Caleb opened his mouth to press further, but the chief's words lingered in the air, heavy and unsettling. The fog drifted between them, winding through the low branches and curling around ancient stones that jutted up from the earth like forgotten sentinels. The burial grounds seemed to pulse with a quiet energy, the kind that comes from centuries of remembrance, of stories layered upon one another like sediment. He sensed there was more to be said, but he also knew Standing Bear was not the kind of man who would be rushed into speaking before he was ready.

"I'll set up a few cameras," Caleb said finally, his tone more subdued as he turned to Kate. "Motion sensors, too. We need to know who—or what—is doing this." He glanced back toward the trees, where the shadows seemed to thicken and breathe with a life of their own.

Kate nodded, her jaw set with determination. "Agreed. And I'll run some tests on the soil and water samples I collected earlier. If there's anything off about the land, it might give us a clue about what's really going on here."

Standing Bear remained silent, watching the two of them as if weighing their resolve. When he spoke again, his voice was calm but firm, a thread of warning woven through the words. "Be careful, Ranger Stone. The forest remembers. It does not forget." Standing Bear's voice dropped to a near whisper. "There are spirits here, forces as old as the roots of these trees. They were not kind even in ancient times, and when provoked, their fury does not fade—it only grows."

The chief's gaze bore into Caleb's, and a shiver crept down his spine. There was an intensity in Standing Bear's eyes that unsettled him, as if the man could see things he couldn't—things that lay just beyond the edges of the known world. "I'll keep that in mind," Caleb replied, though the words felt hollow. He wasn't entirely sure what to make of the warning, nor what exactly the forest was remembering.

As they left the burial grounds, the atmosphere seemed to grow heavier, the air thickening around them with each step. They made their way back to the truck, their footsteps muffled by the damp earth, and Caleb couldn't shake the feeling that they were being watched. It was as if the forest itself was aware of them, and the ancient pines leaned closer, bending and whispering to one another with a language made of rustling leaves and creaking wood. The shadows, now darker and deeper, stretched and shifted in ways that defied reason, as though the ground itself was rippling beneath them.

Caleb cast one last glance back at the burial grounds, where the moss-covered stones stood stark against the encroaching darkness, their silent forms seeming to bear witness to something far beyond his understanding. It was as if they were sentinels of a hidden world, one where time moved differently and the line between the living and the dead was not so easily defined.

"I don't think we're alone out here," Kate whispered, glancing over her shoulder. Her voice was low, barely more than a breath, as though she feared speaking any louder might draw unwanted attention.

Caleb nodded, his gaze sweeping the treeline. "Feels like we're being… watched," he admitted, his own voice hushed. The feeling was more than just a nagging thought; it was a pressure, a weight that seemed to settle over his shoulders, pressing down on him like the forest itself was trying to make him understand its presence.

They reached the truck, but before he climbed in, Caleb took another look around. The forest felt closer now, as if it were leaning in to listen, to watch, to judge. The wind picked up, rustling the trees, but there was something different about the sound—an odd cadence, a whispering beneath the branches that carried on the air, haunting and unsettling.

"Caleb," Kate said, breaking his trance. "Let's get out of here."

He nodded, reluctantly tearing his gaze away from the woods as he climbed into the driver's seat. Kate slid in beside him, closing her door with a soft click. The sound seemed to echo in the silence that had settled over them, an almost ceremonial finality in the action. As they started down the dirt path, Caleb kept glancing at the rearview mirror, half-expecting to see something— someone—standing on the road behind them, watching them leave.

The truck's headlights cut through the thickening fog, illuminating patches of the road as they wound through the dense forest. Shadows flitted across the beams, twisting and contorting in shapes that didn't quite make sense, as though the very air was alive with hidden figures. The silence between him and Kate was heavy, as if neither wanted to break the tenuous calm that had settled over them.

"Do you believe him?" Kate asked finally, her voice soft but piercing through the quiet like a needle. "About the spirits?"

Caleb hesitated, gripping the wheel a little tighter. "I don't know. Part of me thinks he's just trying to keep us out of there. The other part... well, the other part isn't so sure." He glanced at her, searching her expression. "Do you?"

Kate looked down, her fingers tracing idle patterns on the dashboard. "I've spent years studying the land, Caleb. Plants, soil composition, water cycles—they all have energy, a history. It's not just superstition. Sometimes, I think there are things that go beyond what we can measure." She met his gaze, her eyes reflecting a strange mix of wonder and unease. "Maybe there are things out here older than any of us. Things that remember."

They drove in silence for a while, each lost in their own thoughts. As they rounded a bend, the headlights caught a flash of movement just off the road. Caleb slammed on the brakes, his heart hammering as the truck skidded to a halt. For a moment, he saw nothing, the darkness closing in around them once more. But then, just at the edge of the light, something shifted—a shadow, tall and thin, almost humanoid in shape but somehow wrong, as though it were made from smoke and darkness.

"Did you see that?" Kate's voice was barely a whisper, her eyes wide with fear.

Caleb nodded, his pulse pounding in his ears. He strained to see, but whatever it was had already slipped back into the depths of the forest, leaving only the faintest hint of movement in the shadows. The trees stood silent, their branches swaying in the breeze, but the feeling of being watched had intensified, coiling around him like a vice.

"Let's just keep moving," he said, his voice tight. He pressed down on the accelerator, and the truck lurched forward, leaving the spot—and whatever lurked within it—behind. But the tension didn't lift; if anything, it grew sharper, more acute, as though something was following them, slipping through the trees just out of sight.

The Whispering Pines were more than just a place; they were alive in a way that transcended the physical. There was an energy here, something ancient and unyielding, that pulsed beneath the soil and through the roots of the trees. It was waiting, watching, biding its time. For what, Caleb didn't know. But a growing part of him feared that when the truth finally emerged from the shadows, it would not come quietly.

As they left the forest and the road widened, Caleb felt the weight ease just a little, but he knew in his gut that this wasn't over. Whatever was stirring in these woods, it wasn't done with them yet. And neither, he realized, was he done with it.

Beneath the Shadows

The mist hung low over Whispering Pines, curling around the gnarled trunks and clinging to the twisted branches like a restless ghost reluctant to leave. Dawn's first light struggled to pierce the thick canopy overhead, sending pale fingers of sunlight straining through the dense mesh of leaves and pine needles. It was a feeble attempt; the forest swallowed the light, drank it in as if it were nothing more than a fleeting illusion. The air was crisp, almost painfully cold, biting at Caleb Stone's skin with a sharpness that seemed to sink through his clothes, seeping down to his bones. His breath puffed out in pale clouds, lingering briefly in the frigid air before vanishing like a whisper.

Caleb's boots crunched over the damp forest floor, crushing brittle twigs and dried pine needles beneath his weight. Each step seemed to resonate in the eerie stillness, the sound swallowed by the thick fog that clung to the earth. His hands tightened around the worn leather straps of his backpack, as if drawing strength from the familiar feel of the rugged material, as he pressed deeper into the woods. His movements felt slower, each step heavier than the last, weighed down by the crushing revelations of the previous night that gnawed at his mind like hungry wolves.

The forest felt alive—more than alive. It was as if it were watching him, its awareness lurking in the rustling of the wind through the trees and the faint whispering that seemed to come from nowhere and everywhere at once. The ancient pines loomed overhead, their branches twisting like bony fingers, curling inward as if reaching for him or perhaps for something hidden within the shadows. He could almost sense the forest's age, an ancient presence that pulsed in the air like an old, secret rhythm. There was an energy here, simmering just beneath the surface like embers in a fire that refused to die, and with it came an overwhelming feeling that the very earth beneath his feet was breathing—steady, measured, as though it had secrets of its own.

Standing Bear's words echoed relentlessly in Caleb's mind, a refrain that seemed to cling to him as stubbornly as the mist: *The forest remembers. It does not forget.* It was an ominous reminder, an unsettling truth that hung over him like a shadow, growing darker and heavier with each passing day. What had begun as a simple job—a quiet escape from a past that still haunted him—had turned into something else, something darker, as if the forest itself were testing him, beckoning him to confront things long left buried.

The weight of his history pressed against his chest, each breath tinged with memories he had tried to lock away. He had seen too much in his time as a sheriff's deputy: the violence of desperate men, the dull-eyed despair of the bereaved, and the creeping madness that could infect even the most ordinary lives. Yet, none of those encounters had prepared him for this place, for Whispering Pines, where reality and legend bled together, indistinguishable in the dim light that filtered through the canopy. It was as if the boundaries of the world blurred here, the lines dissolving like a charcoal sketch beneath a relentless rain.

A chill ran down Caleb's spine as he glanced over his shoulder, half-expecting to catch sight of a shadow slipping between the trees, or a figure watching him from a distance. But there was nothing—only the unbroken silence and the thick mist curling around the trunks. The trail ahead seemed to twist and disappear into the fog, winding its way through the pines like a serpent, leading him deeper into the heart of the unknown. He could feel the forest closing in around him, the towering trees encircling him in a slow, deliberate embrace, as if to remind him that there was no turning back.

Above him, the call of a lone raven echoed through the forest, its caw cutting through the heavy air like a jagged blade. It was the only sound in the silence, a reminder that life still stirred amid the gloom. Caleb's gaze drifted upward, following the bird's flight as it disappeared into the swirling mist. For a moment, he wondered if the raven was a messenger, a harbinger of what awaited him in the depths of Whispering Pines. Or perhaps it was a warning, a reminder that the forest was not simply a place, but a force—ancient and alive, holding onto its memories with a grip as unyielding as time itself.

Caleb pressed on, the scent of damp earth and pine sap filling his lungs as he ventured deeper into the woods. The path grew narrower, swallowed by the encroaching foliage, and the feeling of being watched did not wane. If anything, it grew stronger, the weight of unseen eyes pressing against his skin. It was as though the forest itself whispered to him, the murmur of leaves stirring on the breeze carrying fragments of words that hovered just out of reach, teasing the edge of his consciousness.

But Caleb wasn't here for legends or ghosts—at least, that's what he kept telling himself. He was here for answers, for truths that had remained hidden for far too long. Yet with every step, it became harder to separate the truth from the tales whispered around campfires, from the stories scrawled on faded maps. The deeper he ventured, the more he felt the forest's grip tighten, pulling him in with a kind of dark, ancient familiarity that was almost welcoming.

The forest remembers. It does not forget.

The words echoed in his mind again, an undeniable truth that made the hair on the back of his neck stand on end. It was as if the woods were trying to speak to him, trying to tell him something about himself that he wasn't ready to hear. And as Caleb continued his solitary march into the heart of Whispering Pines, he couldn't shake the feeling that whatever waited for him there was not only something ancient, but something deeply personal— something that had been waiting for him all along.

The signs had been there from the start: ritualistic mutilations of wildlife, cryptic symbols carved into the trunks of ancient trees, and a growing list of unexplained deaths—each more gruesome than the last. Caleb had seen strange things before, but this was different. There was a methodical cruelty behind these acts, a dark purpose threading them together. Someone—or something—was sending a message, though whether it was a warning, a threat, or an invitation to something far worse, he couldn't yet tell.

It wasn't poachers or reckless hunters fooling around. Caleb had encountered their kind before; he knew the careless damage they left in their wake. But here, in Whispering Pines, the damage wasn't careless. It was calculated. Deliberate. Whatever lurked in these woods was old and patient, with a darkness that seemed to seep into the very marrow of the land, saturating it like blood into soil.

His radio crackled to life, startling him out of his thoughts and breaking the heavy silence that pressed in from all sides. "Caleb," Kate's voice came through, steady but edged with urgency, "I'm at the north perimeter. You need to see this."

He quickened his pace without hesitation, the underbrush crunching beneath his boots, dry twigs snapping underfoot. His senses sharpened with each stride as he moved deeper into the woods, the air growing thicker, the canopy above closing in. The daylight was thin here, its weak fingers of light barely piercing the dense web of branches. Ahead, he could see Kate's silhouette emerging through the haze of morning mist, standing still and tense, her back turned to him. As he drew closer, he saw the pallor of her face, the wide-eyed look that betrayed her shock. She motioned toward a clearing just beyond the tree line, her gaze distant and haunted.

When Caleb stepped into the clearing, a cold dread tightened around his chest, constricting his breath. There, in the center, loomed a towering wooden effigy, its grotesque limbs splayed out like some unholy sentinel. It stood at least ten feet high, constructed from branches, twisted vines, and bones—both animal and human. The fetid stench of decay clung to the air, a sickly-sweet odor that turned his stomach. Ragged animal pelts hung from its limbs, fluttering in the faint breeze like macabre flags. The effigy's crude face, fashioned from bark and dried sinew, stared blankly out into the forest, its hollow eyes fixed as though it had been standing there since time immemorial. Beneath its feet lay a ring of stones, each one etched with the same jagged spiral symbol that had plagued Caleb's dreams for weeks, its meaning elusive but terrifying.

The air around the altar was different here—charged, as if the very atmosphere hummed with a dark energy that prickled against the skin like static before a lightning strike, carrying the faint odor of something foul, like decay mixed with sulfur. It reminded him of the moments before a thunderstorm, when the sky would grow heavy and dark, and the world would hold its breath, waiting for the first crack of lightning.

"This isn't just a message," Kate said, her voice breaking the silence, though it trembled with the effort to keep steady. "This is an altar. A place of… offering."

Caleb stepped closer, his jaw tightening as his eyes roamed over the sinister structure. The way the bones were woven into the wood, the arrangement of the stones, the symbols—they all carried a dark meaning that seemed just out of reach. "What the hell is going on here, Kate?" he muttered, his voice low and rough. "This isn't poachers, and it sure as hell isn't some prank."

Kate shook her head, her gaze still fixed on the effigy. "Standing Bear warned us," she said, her voice barely above a whisper. "He told us there were forces at work here—something ancient, tied to the land itself. We need to take him seriously, Caleb."

Caleb's eyes narrowed, a spark of skepticism flaring up even as a shiver traced down his spine. "Are you suggesting this is some kind of… ancient curse come to life?" he shot back, frustration edging into his voice. "That we're dealing with spirits and folklore?"

"I don't know," Kate replied, a note of helplessness in her tone as her gaze drifted back to the effigy's hollow eyes, which seemed to stare right through her. "But we can't ignore the pattern. The symbols, the deaths, the… altars. It's all connected, and if we don't figure out how, more people are going to die."

Caleb turned his gaze back to the clearing, as he scanned the dark treeline. There was a presence here—something malevolent and old, lingering just beyond the edge of perception. It was as though the very ground beneath his feet vibrated with a dark, ancient energy that pulsed through the roots and soil like a heartbeat. He could feel it now more than ever: the shadows that stretched between the trees seemed to twist and bend, reaching out with dark fingers, as though the forest itself sought to drag him in, its whispers growing louder, now almost like voices—a chorus of the lost, calling him to join them.

"Let's get some pictures," he said at last, reaching for the camera in his pack. "And we need to talk to Standing Bear again. If he knows anything about what's happening, now's the time to share." His voice was steady, but there was a new determination in it, a resolve hardening within him like tempered steel. They needed answers, and they needed them fast.

As they moved through the motions of documenting the scene, Caleb's unease grew. He could feel the forest watching them, a hundred unseen eyes peering out from the depths of the shadows. He glanced over his shoulder, his eyes scanning the dark spaces where the morning light struggled to reach, and for a moment, he thought he saw movement—a flicker of something just beyond the edge of his vision. He froze, his breath catching in his throat, and narrowed his gaze, straining to see what lurked in the darkness. But the moment passed, and the shadows remained still, as if holding their breath. Just the trees, ancient and silent, bearing witness to whatever horror had unfolded here.

Kate approached, her voice low, almost hesitant. "There's something else you should know," she said, her eyes flicking toward the effigy before meeting his. "I ran tests on the water samples from the burial grounds. There's a high concentration of heavy metals in the soil—levels that shouldn't be there."

Caleb frowned, the new information adding to the web of questions tightening around them. "Contamination? Could that explain the animal deaths? The strange behavior we've been seeing?"

"It's possible," she replied, "but it doesn't explain everything. It doesn't explain the symbols, the effigy, or the bodies."

He nodded slowly, his gaze drifting back toward the twisted wooden figure looming in the clearing. "Then we need to keep digging," he said, his voice firm, his determination solidifying with every word. "Whatever's going on here, it's not just about poachers or logging rights. It's about something deeper, something older."

They began their trek back through the forest, an uneasy silence settling between them like a thick fog. As they moved, the woods seemed to close in, the shadows lengthening with each step, creeping ever closer. The path wound through thick brambles and ancient trees, whose gnarled limbs reached out like skeletal hands, as if trying to pull them into the dark. The chill in the air deepened, and Caleb felt it again—a presence that lingered just out of sight, watching them from the gloom. It was as if the land itself had awakened, stirred by their trespasses, its ancient memory rippling with each new discovery.

And somewhere, deep in the darkness between the trees, something waited—a patient hunger that had endured the passage of time, biding its time until now. Caleb could feel it, lurking at the edge of awareness, a whisper that grew louder the deeper they ventured into the heart of Whispering Pines. Whatever it was, it was awake… and it wasn't going to rest until it had been heard.

Above them, the forest canopy swayed gently in the breeze, and the distant call of a crow pierced the silence like a cry from a world long forgotten. It was a place where the lines between reality and myth blurred, where the earth held secrets as old as time itself, and where the past refused to remain buried. Caleb and Kate walked on, their footsteps echoing through the woods, carrying with them the weight of things unseen and the knowledge that whatever lay ahead was far more dangerous than they had ever imagined.

The Hollow Roots

The forest loomed under a thick, oppressive sky, its canopy casting an unnatural darkness over the path. Tendrils of mist snaked between the trees, clutching at the branches like ghostly fingers, and the light filtering through was a muted gray, starved of warmth. A damp, metallic scent hung in the air, blending with the sharp tang of pine and the subtle decay of autumn leaves blanketing the forest floor.

Far overhead, crows circled in uneasy silence, as though even the birds sensed something was amiss. The trees here seemed older, denser, and the gnarled roots twisted over one another in tangled webs, forming a labyrinth across the ground. The forest felt like it was breathing, each rustling branch and shifting shadow pulsing with something ancient and watchful.

Caleb felt the weight of the land pressing down, a thick, invisible force that slowed his steps and seeped into his bones. The whispers seemed to cling to him, rustling from somewhere beyond sight, as if the earth itself was murmuring secrets, too low to hear yet too loud to ignore.

It was in this dense, haunting silence that Caleb and Kate moved forward, each step echoing against the quiet in a way that made Caleb's skin prickle.

Caleb trudged behind Kate, the forest still gripping at his consciousness. The presence—dark, ancient, and gnawing—seemed to hum through the roots beneath his feet, like a vibration in his bones. Each step felt heavier, as though the land itself resisted his movement, pulling him back, as if it knew something they didn't. Their boots crunched on the pine needles, but it was the whispers of the forest that gnawed at Caleb's mind. It felt as though the very trees were watching, mocking them with unseen secrets.

Kate stopped abruptly. Caleb nearly walked into her.

"I think we're close to something," she murmured, her eyes scanning the dense shadows ahead. She adjusted the straps of her pack, her voice taut with tension, though still determined. "Something bigger than we realized."

Caleb wiped the back of his neck, damp with cold sweat. "I don't like this," he muttered under his breath. His gaze swept over the twisted trees, gnarled branches, and the thickening fog that crawled over the forest floor like a predator stalking them. "We need to talk to

Standing Bear again. There's more to this—there has to be. I don't think we have the full picture yet."

"Agreed," Kate responded, but her tone faltered, betraying doubt. She cast a glance over her shoulder at him, her eyes hard but worried. "But are we sure we'll like the answers?"

Caleb's jaw tightened. "I don't think we'll have much of a choice."

As they ventured deeper, the trees seemed to close in on them, the once clear path now a suffocating tunnel of branches and undergrowth. The air grew colder, so cold that Caleb could see his breath in the thin beams of fading sunlight that pierced the thick canopy. The light was disappearing fast, swallowed by the fog and the dense branches overhead, like skeletal fingers reaching down.

The air was thick—heavy. Each breath felt damp, as though inhaling the earth itself, mingling with the scent of rotting leaves and something faintly metallic, sharp on Caleb's tongue. He tried to swallow the taste away, but it clung, persistent.

The forest had grown unnervingly quiet. The distant call of the crow that had followed them, screeching from treetop to treetop, was gone. The silence was too complete, a silence Caleb recognized. It was the quiet of a hunter—predatory, suffocating. He had been hunted before.

"Do you feel that?" he asked, his voice low but tight.

Kate didn't answer immediately. She just nodded, her eyes narrowed as she peered ahead. "Yeah... Something's wrong. Too quiet." She reached for the hunting knife strapped to her thigh, her fingers brushing the hilt as though it might offer some comfort.

Caleb scanned the trees, his hand resting on the grip of the pistol tucked under his jacket. "I don't think we're alone anymore."

The trees seemed to shift, shadows moving just beyond the edges of their vision. He could feel it—a presence, or multiple presences—hidden but near. Watching. Stalking.

"There's something up ahead," Kate whispered, so quietly he almost didn't hear her. Her breath was shallow, her eyes locked on something in the distance, just beyond the fog.

Caleb followed her gaze, squinting through the mist. He couldn't see anything distinct, but there was a shadow, larger than the trees, looming just out of reach. His skin prickled.

"We should fall back," Caleb said, his voice a hushed growl. "Whatever it is, we're not ready."

Kate shook her head, her hand tightening on her knife. "We need to know. We can't leave now."

The silence pressed in on them, broken only by the sound of their own breaths. Caleb's heart pounded in his chest, a drumbeat of unease that matched the pulsing energy of the forest around them. Every instinct screamed at him to retreat, but something else— something darker—pulled him forward, towards whatever was waiting in the shadows.

Suddenly, the fog ahead shifted, parting slightly as if disturbed by something massive moving within it.

Caleb staggered upright, fighting the dizziness that pulsed through his skull, and pulled Kate to her feet. Her hand gripped his arm tightly, her face pale against the dark, shifting fog around them.

"Caleb," she whispered, barely able to keep her voice steady, "we shouldn't be here. Whatever this is… it doesn't want us here."

He nodded, but he couldn't tear his gaze away from the hole. The darkness seemed alive, pulsing with a cold, unearthly energy. Beneath the hollow hum, he thought he could almost hear faint, desperate whispers, as if hundreds of voices were trying to claw their way up from the abyss.

"What's down there?" he wondered aloud, his voice sounding distant even to himself.

Kate shivered and glanced around, eyes darting through the shadows. "Something's wrong here, Caleb. It feels… cursed."

The air around them grew thicker, almost viscous, making every breath an effort. The fog seemed to cling to their skin, pressing in from all sides. Caleb's pulse quickened, the adrenaline fueling his every instinct to flee, but something held him there—an unshakable urge to know what lay at the bottom of that pit.

Kate must have sensed his hesitation. "Caleb, we need to go. Now." She gave his arm a tug, desperation in her voice. "There's something… I don't know, something watching us."

He looked at her, and for a second, the words hung in the air, heavy with a meaning neither of them could articulate. There was no sound, no movement in the trees, and yet he could feel it—a presence, vast and ancient, observing them from the shadows.

"Just a minute," he whispered, crouching low to peer over the edge of the chasm. His hand scraped against the brittle soil, and he pressed his fingers into the earth, feeling its coldness seep into his skin. The tremors beneath him were subtle but steady, like a dormant beast stirring from a deep sleep.

Kate shifted uneasily behind him, her eyes fixed on the hole. "Caleb... please."

Ignoring her for the moment, he took his flashlight from his belt and aimed it into the pit. The beam barely penetrated the darkness, swallowed up by an inky void that seemed to pull the light in. But then, something caught his eye—a glint of movement, deep within the chasm.

Caleb squinted, trying to focus. "There's something down there," he murmured, almost to himself.

"What do you see?" Kate asked, inching closer despite her obvious fear.

"It's... I don't know. It looked like metal... or bone." His voice dropped as he caught another glimpse—a flicker of something white, almost skeletal, vanishing as quickly as it appeared. The shadows shifted, and for a second, he thought he saw a shape, long and coiled, moving just beneath the surface.

"Bones?" Kate's voice was barely a whisper, her face paling even more. "Caleb, this isn't—"

But she never finished. A sudden blast of icy wind tore through the forest, cutting through the fog and whipping past them like a banshee's wail. The trees creaked and groaned, their branches reaching toward the pit as if drawn by some invisible force. The humming from the chasm grew louder, resonating through Caleb's body until he thought his bones might shatter.

Kate stumbled back, her eyes widening with terror. "Caleb, please! We need to get out of here. Now!"

But before he could respond, the ground beneath them lurched again, harder this time. Caleb fell to his knees, gripping the soil as the earth shook violently. The air grew colder, and the low, guttural growl from the chasm deepened, rising into a chilling roar that seemed to come from the depths of the world itself.

Something was rising.

A figure—twisted and shadowed—began to take shape within the pit, slowly clawing its way up from the darkness. Caleb's mind struggled to make sense of it, to discern whether it was solid or smoke. Its form was strange, almost serpentine, with gnarled limbs and a face that shifted, flickering between hollow sockets and a blank, eyeless visage.

Kate screamed, yanking Caleb back to his senses. She grabbed his arm and pulled, hard, dragging him away from the edge as the figure rose higher, its shadow stretching out toward them like a claw.

"Run!" she shouted, and they bolted, stumbling over roots and rocks, desperate to put distance between themselves and the pit. The ground quaked beneath their feet, and the fog thickened, swirling around them like a living thing.

They barely made it a few yards before another tremor hit, and they tumbled to the ground, gasping for air. Caleb looked back, his heart pounding as he caught a final glimpse of the chasm, now glowing with an eerie, unnatural light.

The shadowed figure hovered at the edge, its hollow face turned toward them. For a moment, Caleb thought it was watching, studying them, as if weighing their worth. Then, without warning, it let out a deafening scream—a sound that ripped through the forest, echoing off the trees and chilling them to the bone.

Caleb forced himself to his feet, pulling Kate up beside him. "We have to keep moving!"

They stumbled forward, their breaths ragged, the forest around them seeming to close in. The fog thickened, coiling around them like a vice, and the shadows stretched longer, darker, as if the trees themselves were reaching out to hold them back.

At last, they burst through the treeline, collapsing onto the open ground as the forest fell silent behind them.

Caleb lay there, chest heaving, his mind reeling from the terror they had just escaped. Beside him, Kate clutched at her chest, her eyes wide and unblinking as she stared back at the woods.

"What… what was that?" she whispered, her voice shaking.

Caleb swallowed, his throat dry. He didn't have an answer. All he knew was that whatever they had seen in that pit—whatever ancient, malevolent thing lay buried beneath the roots of the forest—it was watching them now. And it wasn't done with them yet.

"Get up!" he shouted, grabbing Kate's arm and pulling her to her feet. The ground shuddered again, and a crack began to spread from the hole, snaking its way toward the trees.

"What the hell is happening?!" Kate's voice was high with panic as she stumbled after Caleb.

"We have to go! Now!" Caleb's words were edged with terror. He cast a glance back at the dark pit. The noise—no, the voice—was louder now, almost a chant, but in a language he couldn't understand. A wave of icy dread washed over him as the realization hit him like a punch to the gut.

It wasn't just a hole. It was a doorway. Something was down there. And it was waking up.

"We need to find Standing Bear," Caleb said breathlessly, his mind racing. "He'll know what to do."

"Standing Bear?" Kate's voice was almost a scream as she struggled to keep up. "We don't have time for that!"

Another tremor shook the ground beneath them, and they both stumbled, barely managing to stay on their feet. Caleb's heart raced as he pulled Kate toward the trees. The forest seemed to shift around them, the trees creaking and groaning as if they were alive, bending to block their path.

"Go!" Caleb urged, his voice tight with fear. He pushed her forward, his eyes darting back to the pit. The dark chasm seemed to pulse with energy, the air vibrating with it.

Then, from deep within the hole, came a voice. It was faint at first, but grew louder, more distinct. The words were incomprehensible, but the tone sent chills down Caleb's spine. It wasn't a warning—it was a promise.

Something was coming.

Caleb's blood ran cold as he grabbed Kate's arm, dragging her through the thickening forest. The trees seemed to close in on them, their branches clawing at their clothes, their roots tripping them as they ran. The whispers followed them, chasing them into the darkness.

"We need to get out of here," Kate gasped, her voice shaking.

"I know!" Caleb's breath came in short, panicked bursts. He could feel the forest pressing in, the oppressive energy clinging to his skin.

Just as they broke through the trees, a final tremor shook the earth. Caleb risked one last glance over his shoulder. The pit had grown wider, the darkness yawning like an open maw, as if the forest itself was being swallowed whole.

Whatever was down there was no longer asleep. And it wasn't going to stay buried for long.

"We're not safe here," Caleb muttered, more to himself than to Kate. He tightened his grip on her wrist, his mind racing. He couldn't shake the feeling that they were already too late. The dark forest around them seemed to come alive, the shadows stretching, following them like predators hunting their prey.

They didn't stop running, not even when the whispers faded into the distance. Not even when the trees grew still. Because Caleb knew, deep down, that this was only the beginning.

Whatever they had disturbed... was coming for them.

The Hollow Between

The air around them felt electrified as the tremors subsided, leaving a stillness that was even more unsettling than the shaking earth. Caleb's heart pounded in his chest, the pulse echoing in his ears as he steadied Kate with a firm hand. Her breathing was fast, shallow, and her eyes were wide with panic, darting from the now-widening pit back to him.

"This is it," Caleb whispered again, the weight of realization pressing down on him. "This is where it starts."

The words hung in the air like a curse, their meaning too heavy for the moment. He glanced at Kate, her face pale under the canopy's filtered light, the looming darkness of the pit behind them a constant reminder that something ancient had awakened. His mind raced, fragments of Standing Bear's cryptic warnings swirling like leaves in a storm.

"We can't just run," Kate said, her voice trembling but defiant. "If we don't figure this out—if we don't stop it—whatever is down there will keep coming."

Caleb nodded, but every instinct screamed at him to leave. He had seen enough in his time as a sheriff's deputy to know that sometimes the best you could do was survive, but this felt different. It wasn't just about them anymore; the very air was thick with anticipation, as if the forest itself was bracing for something monumental. Something catastrophic.

He could still feel the hum beneath his feet, that rhythmic, unsettling vibration that had started in the pit and now seemed to pulse through the forest, resonating in his bones. The air felt charged, heavy with the promise of something dark and unforgiving.

"We need Standing Bear," Caleb said finally, breaking the oppressive silence between them. "He knows what this is. He can help us stop it."

Kate stared into the distance, her gaze fixed on the path they had just sprinted down, now thick with mist and shadows. "If we can even get to him in time…"

A sudden crack of wood snapped both of their attention back to the forest behind them. The trees groaned under an invisible weight, their branches twisting unnaturally as if they were being bent by a force neither of them could see. The ground trembled again, just slightly, but enough to remind them of the power lurking beneath their feet.

Caleb's hand tightened around Kate's arm, his knuckles white with tension. "We don't have a choice. We move now." His voice was firm, but there was a flicker of uncertainty in his eyes.

Kate yanked her arm free, glaring at him with a fierceness that belied the fear in her eyes. "You always say that! 'No choice, keep moving.' What if moving is exactly what it wants?" Her voice trembled, her frustration uncontainable as they stumbled forward. Each step felt like a battle; roots wound up from the earth like skeletal fingers, and branches slashed at their skin with unnatural precision, as if the forest itself was determined to block their escape.

The thick canopy above swallowed every fragment of moonlight, casting the ground in a dusky haze, and the air was thick with the smell of wet earth and decay. Shadows flickered at the edge of their vision, shifting with their every step, and the damp leaves beneath them squelched as if the ground was breathing.

Caleb ducked under a low-hanging branch, gritting his teeth. "Stop questioning everything, Kate! We don't have time for this right now," he hissed, his tone sharper than he intended, a tremor of desperation threading through his words.

"Maybe we should've made time!" she shot back, her voice piercing through the dense silence around them. She stumbled over an exposed root, catching herself against a tree, her breath ragged. "Maybe if we'd actually thought this through, we wouldn't be running for our lives—again! You don't get it, do you, Caleb? This thing... it's herding us."

Caleb's jaw clenched as he ignored her, every nerve focused on moving forward. But her words pressed on him, sinking in like the thorns that snagged his clothes. What if she was right? What if running was exactly what this thing—or whatever dark power twisted the forest—wanted?

Kate, watching him closely, sensed his hesitation. Her eyes narrowed. "You feel it, don't you?" Her voice was barely more than a whisper, but it sliced through the night's silence. "This place—it's alive now. It wants us here, Caleb. It's not just a forest anymore."

He glanced at her, the unease in his gaze mirroring her own, but he forced himself to shake it off. "We have to keep going," he muttered, more to himself than to her, as if saying it aloud could drown out his doubts. His fingers brushed the worn handle of the hunting knife strapped to his side, the only tangible weapon he had against this intangible nightmare.

Suddenly, they broke through a dense thicket, stumbling into an open space shrouded in mist. The fog hung low, swirling in the faint light as if it were alive, rolling back just enough to reveal a narrow clearing. Relief washed over Caleb, fleeting and fragile—until his eyes fell on the structure in its center.

An altar. But this one was different.

Kate's breath hitched. She froze, her eyes widening with a horror that sent a shiver through Caleb's spine. "No… not again."

The altar loomed in the center of the clearing, intricately crafted, unlike the crude piles of stones they'd come across before. This one was forged from bones— fingers and ribs interwoven with twine—and covered in thick layers of packed earth, etched with symbols that seemed to writhe, glowing with a faint, reddish light like embers barely restrained. A palpable, sinister hum pulsed beneath their feet, syncing with the symbols' rhythm, echoing a deep, ancient energy that vibrated through their bones.

Caleb's mouth was dry as he grabbed her hand again, harder this time. "We can't stay here. We have to keep moving." His voice was low, strained, every word pushed through gritted teeth.

"And go where?" she snapped, jerking her hand back. "Look around, Caleb! There's no escape from this." Her voice was taut, teetering between anger and panic, her eyes glistening with unshed tears. "You keep saying we have to keep moving, but you don't know that! What if running is making it worse? What if we're just… walking into its trap?"

He didn't answer. He didn't know how to. Because deep down, he could feel it too—a pull, dark and magnetic, guiding them deeper and deeper into this cursed forest.

Before he could gather his thoughts, the ground began to tremble. A low, guttural sound resonated from the earth, vibrating up through their feet. The hum that had been distant, almost imperceptible, now roared to life, transforming into a deep, resonant growl that echoed through the trees. It wasn't just a sound anymore—it was a voice. It was everywhere, ancient, seething, filled with rage that was almost tangible.

Kate's hand flew to her mouth, her face pale. "Caleb… that's not just noise."

The voice deepened, the growl weaving through words they couldn't understand, like an ancient chant, a warning laced with anger. The trees swayed as if bending to the will of this unseen force, their branches stretching toward the altar, twisted and claw-like. The symbols on the altar brightened, casting a blood-red glow across their faces, illuminating the terror in Kate's eyes.

Caleb's mind raced, heart pounding as the realization settled over him. They weren't just lost—they were trapped. And whatever inhabited this forest had them right where it wanted them.

"We need to go. Now," he whispered, his voice raw, a shiver running down his spine. But even as he spoke, he wasn't sure there was anywhere left to run.

It spoke in the same language they'd heard before, the one that had echoed near the pit, but now it was louder, more forceful. Caleb couldn't understand the words, but the meaning was clear: *they were trespassing.*

Kate backed away from the altar, her face pale. "We woke it up," she whispered, eyes wide with terror. "We woke it up, Caleb."

"No." He grabbed her shoulders, forcing her to look at him. "No, we didn't wake anything up. It was already awake. We just..." His voice trailed off as the realization hit him like a punch to the gut. "We just made it angrier."

Her lips quivered. "What do we do now?"

Before he could answer, the trees around them shuddered violently. From the shadows emerged figures—dark, twisted shapes flickering in and out of the mist like ghosts. They weren't fully corporeal, but their presence was undeniable. Faintly glowing eyes watched them from within the fog, unblinking, predatory.

"Run!" Caleb shouted, pushing Kate forward as the ground beneath the altar cracked open, splitting the earth wide. The noise was deafening—a thunderous roar as the ancient stones buckled, groaning under the weight of secrets buried for centuries. Dust and debris exploded upward, swallowing them in a haze of jagged shadows and shifting earth. Another chasm yawned open before them, wider and darker than the one they had narrowly escaped earlier, its depths unfathomable.

Kate stumbled, her breaths shallow and uneven. Her eyes were wide, fixed on the churning void that seemed to pulse with a life of its own, beckoning them. "We can't outrun this, Caleb! Look at them! Look at it!" Her voice cracked, teetering between terror and a sob as she pointed at the figures emerging through the mist, barely human shapes, more like shadows with intent—hungry, relentless.

"We have to try!" Caleb yelled, his voice raw with desperation as he grabbed her hand and pulled her forward. He felt her resistance, the way her legs buckled, the way fear had rooted her to the spot as if the forest itself was reaching up, binding her to the ground. But even as they ran, he felt it too—the whispers. Low and ancient, they slithered along the edges of his mind, wrapping around his thoughts like vines. The voices grew louder with every step, each word humming through his bones, a warning that prickled along his skin.

Whatever was in that pit… it was waking up. And it was ravenous.

The forest had never seemed so hostile. The twisted branches clawed at them as they passed, grasping at their clothes, dragging against their skin like skeletal fingers. The fog thickened, twisting and curling around them, alive and sentient, watching. Caleb felt something deep in the earth pulse in time with his own heartbeat, each beat echoing louder as if synced with the forest itself.

Kate stumbled again, nearly falling as her foot snagged on a root that seemed to coil around her ankle with sinister intent. "I can't do this!" she screamed, her voice ragged, tears spilling down her face as she fought to keep moving. "We're not going to make it. You know that, don't you? We're just… delaying the inevitable!"

Caleb stopped, the desperation in her voice slicing through him. He spun around, looking into her tear-streaked face, refusing to let the darkness consume them both. "No! Don't say that. We are not giving up. Not now, not ever." His grip on her arm tightened, grounding both of them. "I don't care what's down there or what it wants. We're going to survive this. We have to."

"How?" Her voice dropped to a fragile whisper, heavy with doubt, shaking with fear. "How do you fight something like this? Something that… isn't even… alive?" Her gaze flicked back toward the figures, looming closer, their faces veiled in shadow, shifting and bending with each step.

Caleb clenched his jaw, his eyes narrowing as he looked past her, meeting the gaze of the phantoms encircling them, their eyes dark pools of unfathomable menace. He didn't have an answer. The cold truth clawed at him, digging in, whispering the same fears she'd voiced. They couldn't fight this. They couldn't even understand it. He didn't know if there was any way out, any way to escape.

But he refused to let her see that weakness. He forced a grim smile, a confidence that felt more like a mask he wore for her sake. "We'll figure it out," he lied. "We've made it this far, haven't we?"

They started running again, side by side, but Caleb could feel the weight of his own words bearing down on him, heavier with each step. The forest itself seemed to throb with malevolent intent, the air thick and acrid, clinging to them like smoke. Every footfall sent a shudder through the ground beneath them, as if even the earth itself was part of the chase, urging them deeper, luring them into its grasp.

Behind them, the whispers grew louder, sharper. They had transformed into a chorus—a cacophony of voices speaking in that ancient tongue, words that reverberated through the trees, through the soil, vibrating within him, within his bones. Caleb risked a glance at Kate, who was visibly trembling, her breaths reduced to shallow gasps, each one more labored than the last. Her face was drained, her eyes hollow and vacant with a terror that had rooted itself in her very core.

"Keep going," he urged, his own voice barely a murmur now, not sure if he was talking to her or to himself. "We're not going to die here." He repeated it, like a mantra, clinging to the words even as doubt threatened to tear them from his lips. They had to survive. They had to. He wouldn't let them die here, not like this.

But as they continued, the whispers crescendoed, transforming into a guttural chant that seemed to fill every crevice of the forest. It echoed off the trees, rebounded from the stones, filling their minds with thoughts that weren't their own, fears that went deeper than anything either had ever known. Caleb felt his resolve begin to fray as the words wormed their way into his mind, twisting his thoughts, drowning his determination.

"What if we're already lost?" Kate's voice was barely audible, her words dripping with despair. Her fingers clutched his hand tighter, as if he were the only anchor holding her in this world, the only thing tethering her to the reality she was rapidly losing grip of. "What if… what if this is what it wants? What if this is what we are now?"

Caleb shook his head, gripping her hand even tighter, forcing himself to keep his gaze locked on the path ahead. "No. We're going to make it out. I don't know how, but we're going to make it out." He gritted his teeth, pushing down the fear, refusing to let it show. He had to be strong—for both of them.

They stumbled forward, their bodies bruised and battered, each step a battle against the earth itself. And yet, as they moved, the forest closed in tighter, its branches bending, twisting, reaching. The fog swirled thicker, consuming the path behind them, transforming every step into a journey deeper into darkness, deeper into the unknown.

A low rumble shook the ground, and Caleb felt it—a new chasm tearing open, a monstrous void spreading beneath their feet, as if the forest itself were hungry, as if it yearned to devour them whole. The voices rose, a crescendo of ancient fury, a promise of despair that reverberated through his bones.

The thought clawed its way into his mind, chilling him to the core: *What if they were never meant to escape?*

The Gathering Shadows

The forest lay shrouded in darkness, an ancient expanse of tangled roots and shadowed branches veiled in thickening mist. The air hung heavy, saturated with the scent of damp earth and decaying leaves, a haunting reminder of the forest's relentless cycle of life and death. Above, the sky stretched out in a slate-gray sheet, starless, pressing down upon the land as if withholding something ominous from the trees below. A stillness had settled, broken only by the occasional distant rustle—a cautious stirring, like some unseen creature skirting the edge of the darkness, wary yet watchful.

In the dim light, the Whispering Pines were no longer mere trees but looming silhouettes, their rough bark textured like ancient scars, their twisted branches reaching out like gnarled hands. The mist wove through the trunks, curling around Caleb's boots as he stepped forward, thickening with each breath until it felt as if he was inhaling the very essence of the forest. The chill in the air sharpened, sinking deep into his skin as a low breeze drifted between the trees, carrying with it the faintest scent of pine, mixed with an odd, metallic tang that seemed to come from nowhere—and everywhere.

The forest felt alive, alert, and something in its depths watched him. Caleb could feel it, the weight of unseen eyes following his every movement, the silent whisper of secrets buried deep within the roots. Each step into the shadows pulled him closer to the heart of the unknown, where ancient powers lay dormant, waiting to be stirred from their slumber.

The evening had settled into a somber twilight by the time Caleb arrived at the ranger station, a chill spreading through the Whispering Pines National Park as mist crept over the forest floor. The sky was an endless expanse of steel gray, where thick clouds hung low, smothering the last glimmers of daylight. A dampness saturated the air, turning every breath into a cold, heavy pull that Caleb felt deep in his lungs. The trees stood in clusters, their rough bark darkened by the mist, casting long shadows that blurred together, creating an illusion of movement just at the edge of vision.

The dense pines around the station loomed, their branches knotted and twisted like the fingers of ancient giants, and every gust of wind sent them creaking in uneasy harmony. Caleb could smell the faint, earthy scent of decaying leaves and wet soil mingling with the pungent tang of pine resin—a reminder of the forest's unyielding cycle of life and death.

Inside the ranger station, the air felt stale and closed, weighed down by the scent of unwashed coffee mugs and paper yellowed by the damp. The silence was oppressive, broken only by the low hum of the overhead lights and the occasional crackle of the radio on his desk. Maps were pinned to the walls, illuminated by a dim desk lamp, each marking the places where the forest had given up strange and unsettling secrets. The sharp, erratic red markings spread across the map in a loose spiral, like the heart of a web—and he was caught right in its center.

It was as if the forest was alive with a silent, brooding energy that was just out of reach, thickening the air and setting his nerves on edge. The moment he stepped inside, Caleb could sense it: an expectation, something lurking beneath the surface, waiting for him to make his next move.

Caleb fingers tapped impatiently on the rough wooden desk, a dull echo against the persistent quiet of the ranger station. The air felt thick, stale, and laced with the faint scent of old coffee and musty papers—a combination that had grown familiar over the past months. Caleb had seen gruesome crime scenes before, but the recent discoveries within Whispering Pines gnawed at him differently. He leaned back, rubbing his temples, as if trying to massage clarity into his cluttered mind.

The map on the wall in front of him was marked with red circles, each representing a site of animal mutilation or other unusual activity. He traced the path connecting them with his eyes—an irregular but unmistakable pattern that seemed to form a rough spiral. Caleb frowned, a feeling of unease settling deep in his gut. The more he stared at the pattern, the more he felt as if the spiral itself was mocking him, like a sinister taunt whispered in the dark.

The radio on the desk crackled to life, breaking the oppressive silence. "Caleb, are you there?" Kate's voice came through, the edge in her tone cutting through the static like a knife.

"Yeah, I'm here," he replied quickly, grabbing the radio. "What's going on?"

"Standing Bear called," she said. "He's waiting for you at the ceremonial grounds, east of the ridge. He said it's urgent, and you need to come alone."

Caleb's jaw tightened. The ceremonial grounds were sacred to the local tribe, a place reserved for rituals and spiritual gatherings. Standing Bear's request carried a weight Caleb couldn't ignore, but the urgency of it made him uneasy.

"I'm on my way," he said into the radio, already grabbing his jacket and keys.

The drive to the ceremonial grounds felt longer than it was. The winding dirt road cut through the dense pines, which seemed to close in around him, their dark branches intertwining above like skeletal fingers. The forest was unnervingly quiet, as if holding its breath. Only the occasional rustle of leaves broke the stillness, sending fleeting shivers down Caleb's spine. The headlights of his truck barely pierced the thick fog that settled over the land, making the trees appear as looming shadows, silent witnesses to the darkness that seemed to seep from the very ground.

Caleb paused, his ears straining against the unnerving stillness that blanketed the woods. A faint rustle echoed from somewhere deep within the trees—a sound that seemed out of place in the oppressive quiet. He scanned the dense undergrowth, his eyes darting between the towering pines, where long shadows crept up their trunks like dark, skeletal fingers reaching for the sky. But there was nothing, only shadows shifting lazily under the pale light of the setting sun, as if hiding from his gaze, retreating just out of reach.

The woods stretched endlessly around him, each tree identical to the next, a wall of indistinguishable, silent giants. A dense fog began to unfurl, slipping between the roots and pooling around his boots, a cold, clammy sensation that left his skin prickling with unease. The air grew thick, heavy with the damp scent of moss and rotting leaves, and he felt as though he was breathing in the forest itself—its secrets, its stories, its deaths.

Suddenly, a sharp drop in temperature sent a shiver racing down his spine. The warm, muggy air seemed to evaporate, replaced by an icy chill that hung heavy, as if the forest itself exhaled a breath colder than the grave. Caleb's breath misted visibly before him, lingering like a ghostly vapor. Each inhalation felt sharper, biting, and as he exhaled, his breath dissipated into the fog, swallowed whole by the darkening forest.

Then, a low whisper drifted through the pines, too faint to be words, but unmistakably there—a sound like leaves brushing against each other, except there was no wind. It seemed to come from nowhere and everywhere at once, as if the very air carried the echoes of something old, something watching. The whisper grew, weaving itself around him, pulling him deeper into the forest's shadowed heart. He felt a weight settle on his shoulders, pressing down, urging him to turn back even as he was drawn further in.

"Hello?" Caleb's voice was rough, cutting through the stillness like a blade, shattering the thick silence. His voice sounded foreign, weak, quickly swallowed by the heavy atmosphere, leaving an emptiness that felt thicker than before. He gripped his flashlight tighter, feeling the weight of the darkness pressing against him, a darkness that seemed alive, creeping closer with each breath he took.

Silence fell again, deeper and more suffocating, as if the forest itself had swallowed the sound, refusing to release it. He could feel the trees watching, their branches reaching out with spindly fingers, cloaked in fog, whispering secrets he was never meant to hear. A shadow flickered at the edge of his vision—a figure, or perhaps just a trick of the light. Caleb's pulse quickened, his heart hammering against his ribs. He could feel it now, the unshakable sense of being watched, the weight of unseen eyes following his every movement, tracking him through the trees.

Just as he took a step back, something cracked behind him—a sharp snap, like a twig breaking underfoot. Caleb whipped around, his flashlight beam slicing through the fog, revealing only the empty forest. He swallowed, his throat dry, eyes darting as he searched for any sign of movement.

But there was only the darkness, thick and unyielding, wrapping around him, holding him in its grip.

When Caleb finally reached the clearing, he spotted the faint glow of a bonfire flickering through the trees.

He stepped out of the truck, the chill night air hitting his face like a cold slap. He paused for a moment, taking in the scene before him. Around the fire stood a group of tribal elders, their faces illuminated by the orange glow, their expressions solemn and distant, as if they were looking at something far beyond the flames.

Caleb swallowed, the weight of Standing Bear's words sinking into him. He reached for the pouch, his fingers brushing against its rough fabric, woven from thick fibers that smelled of earth and smoke. The sensation grounded him, even as his mind swirled with questions. He could feel the weight of unseen eyes around him, lurking just beyond the firelight, watching, waiting.

"What do you expect me to do with this?" Caleb asked, voice softer now, the skepticism of before having dissipated, replaced by something closer to fear.

Standing Bear regarded him for a long moment, his face unreadable in the flickering light. "Take it with you wherever you go, as a reminder and a shield. But more importantly," he added, lowering his voice, "remember that you cannot defeat what you do not respect. Approach the forest not as a guardian of the law, but as a humble guest on ancient land."

Caleb wanted to laugh it off, to chalk up Standing Bear's words to superstition, but something in the chief's eyes held him captive. It was like looking into the depths of an ancient well, a place so dark and profound that even the sun's light couldn't penetrate it. Caleb had never felt anything quite like it—a feeling of being drawn into something beyond himself, a current pulling him into the dark waters of a hidden world.

A rustle from the edge of the clearing snapped him out of his thoughts, and he turned to see a shadow slipping between the trees. The firelight caught it just for a second—a flash of pale fur, a glint of amber eyes, a large, sinewy shape moving silently through the brush. Caleb blinked, wondering if his mind was playing tricks on him, but Standing Bear's gaze followed his, his expression unchanging.

"It is one of the forest's guardians," Standing Bear said in a hushed tone. "They have been watching you since you first entered the park. They sense your conflict, your disbelief, and your fear."

Caleb felt a prickling sensation at the back of his neck. "Guardians?" he repeated, his voice barely a whisper. "You mean... animals?"

"Animals, yes," Standing Bear replied, "but also something more. They are spirits given form, protectors of the balance we have disrupted. Some call them shadows of the past; others see them as omens. But they do not belong to the world of men." He glanced back at Caleb. "They are here to remind you of that."

The wind picked up again, colder this time, biting through Caleb's jacket and sending a shiver down his spine. He clenched his jaw, forcing himself to meet Standing Bear's unwavering gaze. "If these... guardians are so powerful, why do they need us to protect the forest? Why rely on people like me, or even the tribe, to maintain the balance?"

Standing Bear's lips pressed into a thin line. "Because even they have limits. When humans began to strip the land, to hunt without purpose, they disturbed a balance that has been held for centuries. The guardians act in subtle ways, influencing thoughts, shaping dreams. But they cannot undo the damage of greed or carelessness. That is why they called you here, Caleb—because you, too, have a role in this story."

Caleb's hand tightened around the pouch, his resolve hardening. He didn't fully understand the forces at play here, but he couldn't deny the weight of Standing Bear's words, the sense of something vast and unseen brushing up against the edges of his reality. As he stood in that clearing, surrounded by elders, chants, and offerings to powers older than memory, a small part of him began to believe—or, if not believe, at least accept—that there was more to this place than he could explain.

The elder who had handed over the pouch began to chant once more, his voice deep and resonant, each syllable carrying an ancient rhythm. Caleb felt it vibrate through his bones, pulling him deeper into the moment, into the heartbeat of the forest around them. Other voices joined in, creating a wave of sound that washed over him, hypnotic and haunting.

As the chanting continued, Caleb noticed something strange. The flames of the fire were no longer dancing erratically; instead, they were still, almost frozen, as if held in some supernatural stasis. The air grew thick and heavy, pressing against his chest, making it hard to breathe. Shadows began to gather at the edges of his vision, dark shapes that writhed and twisted like smoke, coalescing into forms that seemed to pulse with life.

One of the shapes, larger than the others, took the form of a wolf—its eyes glowed a spectral white, and its fur seemed to ripple as if caught in a breeze only it could feel. The wolf's gaze locked onto Caleb, and he felt a surge of energy course through him, filling him with both fear and a strange, exhilarating strength.

The wolf tilted its head, and Caleb could have sworn it nodded, a silent acknowledgment, a promise that it was watching. Then, as quickly as it had appeared, it faded into the darkness, leaving behind only the faint smell of wet earth and pine.

The chanting stopped, and silence reclaimed the clearing. Caleb felt like he'd just awoken from a dream, disoriented and unsure of what he'd just witnessed. Standing Bear stepped forward, placing a hand on Caleb's shoulder, grounding him with the warmth of his touch.

"Remember what you have seen tonight, Caleb. The guardians do not show themselves lightly. They have chosen you as their ally, for now. But make no mistake," Standing Bear's voice grew stern, "if you fail to heed their warnings, they will not hesitate to treat you as an intruder."

Caleb nodded; his throat tight. He wanted to ask a hundred questions, but the weight of the experience had left him speechless. He glanced back at the forest, half-expecting to see the spectral wolf again, watching him from the shadows. But the clearing was empty, silent, the only movement coming from the smoldering embers of the fire.

Finally, he managed to find his voice. "I don't know if I believe in spirits, Chief," he said quietly. "But I'll protect this place... whatever it takes."

Standing Bear gave a solemn nod. "Belief is not required, Caleb. Only respect." He let his hand fall away, leaving Caleb alone with the pouch and the silence. The chief's parting words lingered in the cold air like an echo, one that Caleb knew he would carry with him wherever he went.

As he turned to leave the clearing, a distant howl pierced the night—a sound both mournful and defiant, a call that seemed to carry with it the weight of the land itself. Caleb paused, listening, feeling a strange kinship with the voice in the darkness. It was a warning, a reminder, and a promise all in one. And as he made his way back to his cabin, he couldn't shake the feeling that his journey had only just begun.

"I don't believe in curses or spirits," he said slowly, his voice laced with uncertainty. "But I do believe in danger. And I'll take any help I can get."

Standing Bear handed him the pouch, and Caleb tucked it into his jacket pocket, the small weight feeling strangely heavy. As he did, a sudden rustling came from the trees at the edge of the clearing. Caleb's hand instinctively moved to the gun at his hip, his senses on high alert. The elders remained calm; their eyes trained on the darkness beyond the firelight.

"There is something here," Standing Bear said quietly, his voice barely audible over the crackle of the fire. "It has been watching us."

Caleb squinted into the darkness, his eyes straining to make out any movement. For a moment, he saw nothing but shadows and swaying branches. Then, he caught a glimpse of something—an indistinct figure, just beyond the edge of the light, its shape obscured by the fog. It was tall, broad, and eerily still, as if it were part of the forest itself.

"What is it?" Caleb whispered, his voice tense.

"An old spirit," Standing Bear replied. "One that is not pleased with our presence."

Caleb's grip tightened on the gun, though he knew instinctively that it would be useless against whatever was out there. The figure remained motionless; its form barely visible through the shifting mist. Caleb's heart pounded in his chest, a primal fear gripping him.

And then, as quickly as it had appeared, the figure vanished, swallowed by the darkness. Caleb exhaled slowly, his muscles relaxing slightly, but the sense of unease lingered.

"You have much to learn about this land, Caleb," Standing Bear said, his tone a mix of warning and resignation. "The spirits are not bound by time or space. They do not forget, and they do not forgive."

Caleb nodded slowly, the chief's words echoing in his mind. He had come to Whispering Pines to escape his past, to find some semblance of peace in the wilderness.

But the forest had other plans. It was a living, breathing entity, filled with secrets that refused to stay buried.

As he turned to leave, Caleb felt a strange sense of determination rising within him. He wasn't sure if he believed in spirits or curses, but he knew one thing for certain: he wasn't going to back down. Whatever darkness lay within the depths of Whispering Pines, he was going to confront it—no matter what it took.

The drive back to the ranger station was silent, the thick fog and dense trees closing in around Caleb as if the forest itself were watching his every move. His mind replayed the events at the ceremonial grounds, Standing Bear's warnings, and the haunting chant of the elders. It all felt surreal, like a dream that lingered in the waking world, refusing to fade.

Back at the station, Caleb slumped into his chair, exhaustion washing over him. He pulled the small pouch from his jacket pocket and set it on the desk, staring at it with a mixture of skepticism and curiosity. The weight of the pouch was a tangible reminder of the unseen forces at play in the park, forces that were as mysterious as they were dangerous.

He reached for the phone, dialing Kate's number. She picked up on the third ring, her voice groggy but alert. "Caleb? What's going on?"

"I just got back from the ceremonial grounds," he said, his voice low. "Standing Bear gave me some kind of protection charm. He thinks the spirits are angry, that something's been disturbed."

Kate was silent for a moment, then spoke carefully. "Do you believe him?"

"I don't know," Caleb admitted. "But I can't shake the feeling that there's more to this than just poachers and rituals. There's something deeper, something that's been here long before us."

Kate sighed. "Then we'll have to dig deeper too. I've been working on some theories about the symbols we've found. They're not just random spirals, Caleb. They have meaning—ancient meaning. I think they might be tied to a ritual of summoning or binding."

Caleb's brow furrowed. "Summoning or binding what?"

"That's what we need to figure out," Kate said. "But it's clear that whoever—or whatever—is doing this, they're not done yet."

The words hung in the air like a dark omen, filling the room with a sense of impending danger. Caleb's resolve hardened. He wasn't just fighting poachers or greedy businessmen anymore; he was up against something far older, something that seemed to exist in the very roots of the forest.

As the first light of dawn began to creep through the window, Caleb felt a strange sense of calm. The darkness was vast, and the odds were against him, but he wasn't alone. He had allies, however unlikely they might seem. And he had the land itself—both its danger and its beauty—to guide him.

Caleb knew one thing for certain: the fight was just beginning, and he was ready to face it head-on, no matter how deep the shadows stretched.

The Roar of the Pines

A low, bruised sky hung heavy over Whispering Pines, the oppressive weight of storm clouds pressing down on the ancient forest like a suffocating blanket. The air was thick and damp, carrying the earthy scent of pine and wet soil, mingled with an acrid hint of ozone. Thunder rolled in the distance, a deep, bone-shaking growl that reverberated through the trees as if waking something primal and ancient.

The pines themselves loomed in dark clusters, their trunks twisting and arching like silent sentinels. Branches hung heavy with needles that trembled in the gathering wind, casting long, eerie shadows across the forest floor. In the dimming light, the forest seemed alive, its towering figures and rustling underbrush creating a haunting tableau of shifting shapes and lurking shadows.

Ahead, through the dense maze of trees, a narrow trail wound its way toward the distant cliffs. Along this path, Caleb Stone moved with purpose, his every step sinking into the rain-soaked earth that clung to his boots like a second skin. The trees groaned under the weight of the incoming storm, their branches creaking and straining, and every step was met by the oppressive silence of nature holding its breath.

In the distance, a flash of lightning split the sky, briefly illuminating the darkened outline of the cave—a yawning mouth set in the cliffs, partially hidden by undergrowth and tangled roots. Caleb's heart pounded as he closed in on his target, knowing that within that cave lay not just the evidence of Clyde's crimes but also the future of Whispering Pines.

The storm was merciless, a torrential force that transformed Whispering Pines into a chaotic nightmare. Rain pelted the ground relentlessly, turning the trails into slick, unstable paths. Thunder cracked like a whip overhead, while lightning forked through the black sky, illuminating the forest in stark, jagged bursts. The pines swayed violently, their twisted branches seeming to reach out as if alive, hungry to pull Caleb Stone into the heart of the storm.

Caleb's boots struggled for traction in the mud, but he pressed forward, adrenaline coursing through his veins. Every step brought him closer to the cave, where Roger Clyde and his men were preparing to destroy the evidence of their crimes. Caleb's mind raced. He had to stop them—this wasn't just about saving the land; it was about stopping Clyde's ruthless ambitions and exposing the corruption that had taken root in Whispering Pines.

The cave's outline emerged from the darkness, partially obscured by thick undergrowth and massive, gnarled roots. Caleb spotted Kate Jensen up ahead, a dark figure moving with urgency. Lightning briefly illuminated her face, revealing determination etched in her features. She turned back, shouting over the storm's roar.

"Hurry, Caleb! We're running out of time!"

Caleb nodded, though he doubted she could see him. His grip on his pistol tightened as he crept toward the cave entrance, scanning the shadows. This was it. The culmination of months of investigation, confrontations, and betrayals. He felt the weight of it all in his chest, alongside the familiar, cold resolve that had carried him through dark moments before.

Suddenly, the crack of a gunshot split the air. Caleb dropped to the ground, mud splattering his face as he rolled behind a fallen log for cover. He heard Kate's voice from somewhere nearby.

"Get down, Caleb!"

He crawled forward, keeping low. The storm's fury masked most sounds, but the gunfire was unmistakable— Roger Clyde's men were guarding the cave entrance.

Another shot rang out, this one hitting the trunk of a tree inches from Caleb's head. He cursed under his breath, adrenaline spiking.

A familiar voice called out from the darkness, taunting and filled with disdain. "You really think you can stop this, Stone? You're a fool!"

It was Clyde, his voice cutting through the wind and rain. Caleb felt a surge of anger. "You're the fool, Clyde! You think you can destroy everything and walk away clean?"

Clyde laughed, the sound harsh and hollow. "This land's already dead, Stone. It just doesn't know it yet!"

Caleb's jaw clenched, but before he could respond, Kate's voice came urgently through the darkness. "Caleb! We need to take them out before they set off the explosives inside the cave!"

Caleb knew she was right. He signaled to Kate, then motioned for her to circle around and try to get a clear shot at the men near the cave entrance. He moved slowly, keeping low, his eyes trained on the shifting shadows. The storm's fury was relentless, making visibility difficult, but it also provided cover. He inched closer, his heart pounding.

Then he saw them: two of Clyde's henchmen, positioned at the cave entrance, their rifles aimed into the dark. Caleb raised his pistol and fired twice. One man fell immediately, clutching his shoulder, while the other scrambled for cover. Caleb pressed forward, using the momentary confusion to close the distance.

The second man recovered quickly, returning fire. Caleb felt a searing pain in his side as a bullet grazed him, but he pushed through the pain, firing again. The shot hit its mark, and the man crumpled to the ground. Caleb reached the cave entrance just as Kate emerged from the opposite side, her rifle aimed at the darkness beyond.

"Are you okay?" she asked, her voice tight with concern.

Caleb nodded, wincing as he clutched his side. "I'm fine. Just a scratch. We need to move—Clyde's got more men inside, and they're not going to back down easily."

They entered the cave cautiously, their flashlights cutting through the darkness. The air was damp and stale, the ground uneven and covered with loose rocks. Caleb's heart raced as he scanned the cavern, his senses on high alert. They moved deeper, the sounds of hurried voices and shifting crates echoing from further inside.

Suddenly, a familiar figure stepped into the light— Chief Tom Standing Bear. His face was a mix of anger and desperation, his eyes hard. He held a shotgun, its barrel leveled at Caleb and Kate.

"Drop your weapons," Tom ordered, his voice steady but filled with conflicted resolve.

Caleb's mind reeled. "Chief, what the hell are you doing?"

Tom's grip on the shotgun tightened. "This isn't what I wanted, Stone. But you've given me no choice."

Kate's voice was filled with disbelief. "Tom, this is insane! You can't think this is the way to protect your people!"

Tom's face twisted with pain. "You don't understand. The artifacts… they were our last hope to reclaim what's been taken from us. I did what I had to do."

Caleb felt a surge of anger mixed with betrayal. "You've betrayed everything you claimed to protect, Tom! This land isn't yours to sell!"

The chief's gaze faltered for a moment, but then he steadied himself. "You don't know what it's like to be pushed to the edge, Stone. I was trying to save my people. This was the only way."

Before Caleb could respond, another voice echoed through the cave—Roger Clyde's, cold and commanding.

"Enough of this nonsense. Shoot them, Tom. Or get out of the way."

Clyde emerged from the darkness; his face twisted in a sneer. He held a detonator in one hand, his other clutching a pistol. "You see, Stone? Even the righteous can be bought."

Caleb's heart pounded as he stared at the detonator. "If you set that off, you'll destroy everything—these artifacts, the forest, everything that makes this land sacred!"

Clyde's grin widened. "It's not about the land, Stone. It's about control. I'll erase all the evidence, and you'll be just another dead body in a cave collapse."

Caleb's mind raced. He needed a way to stop Clyde, to reach Tom, and to protect Kate—all while the cave seemed ready to collapse around them. The storm's howls were muffled here, but the walls shook with the occasional thunderous boom from outside.

Tom's hands trembled, the shotgun wavering between Caleb and Kate. His eyes were filled with guilt and desperation. "Roger, this isn't what we agreed—"

Clyde cut him off sharply. "I don't care what you thought we agreed on. This is how it ends."

Kate took a step forward, her voice steady but urgent. "Tom, think about what you're doing! This isn't saving your people; it's destroying everything you believe in!"

Tom's gaze flickered with uncertainty. Caleb saw his chance. "It's not too late, Tom. Drop the gun. Help us stop Clyde. We can fix this—together."

For a moment, it seemed like Tom might lower the shotgun. But Clyde, sensing his hesitation, lunged forward, trying to grab the weapon. In the scuffle, the gun went off, the deafening blast echoing through the cavern.

The air was thick with dust and the acrid smell of gunpowder, making it hard for Caleb to breathe. The dim light from his flashlight flickered, struggling against the gloom of the cave's depths. The walls were jagged and uneven, the rock wet from the storm outside and slick underfoot. Shadows danced ominously, making the cavern feel smaller, as if it were closing in on them with every passing second.

Caleb felt a searing pain in his shoulder and stumbled back, clutching the wound. Blood seeped through his fingers, warm and sticky, as he fought to keep his vision from blurring. His teeth clenched against the agony as he forced himself to stay upright, a mixture of adrenaline and sheer willpower anchoring him to the spot.

"Caleb!" Kate's voice cut through the chaos like a razor, sharp and frantic. She was at his side in an instant, her hands trembling as she reached for his shoulder, trying to assess the injury despite the blood soaking through his jacket. "You're hurt. You need help."

He shook his head, waving her off. "I'm fine," he grunted, though the pain was making it harder to keep his breathing steady. His face was pale, his expression taut, but his eyes held a fierce, unwavering resolve. "We need to stop Clyde. No one else gets hurt because of him."

A few paces away, Chief Tom stood frozen, his gun lowered, his face a mask of horror. His hand trembled, not from the weight of the weapon, but from the shock of what he had just witnessed. The realization that he was standing at the crossroads of duty and betrayal was etched into every line of his face.

"Tom!" Caleb's voice was harsh, desperate, echoing across the cavern walls. "Don't just stand there! We can't let him do this."

Tom's eyes darted between Caleb and Clyde, as if he were trapped in an impossible dilemma, his loyalty to his tribe and his duty as a chief pulling him in opposite directions. But his silence was answer enough. He wouldn't—or couldn't—act.

Caleb's heart sank, but there was no time for hesitation. His gaze shifted to Clyde, who stood a few feet ahead, a man possessed by his own darkness. Clyde's dark eyes glinted with a dangerous mix of triumph and madness, and a twisted smile curled across his lips as he raised his hand, revealing a small black detonator. He wiped a smear of blood from his cheek, his grin growing more sinister.

"You see?" Clyde's voice was low, mocking, each word dripping with malice. "No more heroes, Stone. Just the dead and the forgotten."

With a defiant smirk, he pressed the button on the detonator, expecting a fiery eruption to follow.

Nothing happened.

Clyde's confident expression faltered, confusion clouding his eyes as he pressed the button again, harder this time, his thumb grinding against it with increasing frustration. But still, there was only silence. His face twisted with a flicker of panic, and he glanced back at Caleb, the realization dawning on him that his plan was unraveling.

"You really think I'd let you have the last move, Clyde?" Caleb's voice was tight with pain, but there was a steely edge to it, one that cut through the tension like a blade. "I disabled the detonator when you weren't looking. It's over."

For a moment, Clyde stared at Caleb, his face a mixture of anger and disbelief. But the fury won out, and with a savage growl, he lunged forward, abandoning all semblance of control. He swung wildly, fists crashing toward Caleb, desperate and unrestrained. Caleb, despite the throbbing agony in his shoulder, met Clyde head-on, and the two men collided, tumbling to the ground in a brutal struggle.

They rolled across the uneven, rocky floor, their grunts and labored breaths filling the air. Clyde's fists came down fast and hard, fueled by desperation and unbridled rage. He landed a powerful punch to Caleb's jaw, sending a sharp jolt through him and momentarily disorienting him. But Caleb fought back, planting his good shoulder into Clyde's chest, throwing him off-balance as he grappled for control.

"Caleb, don't let him—" Kate's voice rang out, urgent and filled with worry as she watched the brutal struggle unfold.

Clyde snarled, grabbing a fistful of Caleb's shirt, his knuckles white with the force of his grip. "You think you're better than me?" he spat, his voice filled with venom. "You think you're a hero? You're nothing, Stone. Just a dead man waiting to happen."

But Caleb's gaze never wavered. "Better than you?" he whispered, breathing hard. "I don't have to be better. I just have to be willing to stop you." And with a swift, calculated move, he jabbed his knee into Clyde's abdomen, knocking the wind out of him.

Clyde gasped, his grip loosening, but he wasn't done. With a roar, he twisted free and grabbed a nearby rock, raising it high above his head, ready to bring it down with deadly force. Caleb's eyes locked onto the rock, and for a split second, time seemed to slow. He knew he had to act fast.

In that moment, Kate stepped forward, a fire extinguisher from the nearby equipment in her hands. She swung it with all her strength, the heavy metal canister connecting with the side of Clyde's head with a sickening thud. The impact sent him reeling, and he staggered, the rock slipping from his hand as he crashed to the ground, dazed and bleeding.

Caleb took a shaky breath, relief washing over him as he struggled to sit up, his shoulder screaming in protest. "Nice timing," he managed to say, giving Kate a faint smile.

She dropped the fire extinguisher, her face pale but resolute. "Didn't think I'd stand by and let you get all the fun."

Caleb chuckled, though the sound was strained. He pushed himself to his feet, his gaze drifting to Clyde's prone form. The man's eyes fluttered, barely conscious, his body limp and defeated. Caleb took a moment to catch his breath, feeling the weight of everything they had just been through settling over him.

As the echoes of their struggle faded, Tom finally took a step forward, his face ashen and torn. Caleb looked at him, a mixture of pity and disappointment in his eyes. "It didn't have to end like this, Tom. But now… it's done."

Tom nodded slowly, his shoulders slumping, defeated by the gravity of his choices.

Before Kate could finish, Clyde's hand shot out, grabbing her by the arm and yanking her closer. She stumbled forward, the jagged rocks beneath her scraping her knees as he pulled her tight against him, using her as a human shield. His grip was like iron, and no amount of twisting seemed to break it.

"Stay back!" Clyde's voice was a raw snarl, his eyes wild with desperation. His knife gleamed under the flickering light, pressing against Kate's throat. "I swear, I'll do it."

The cave was eerily silent, save for the echo of his threat. Tom, a step away but frozen with indecision, swallowed hard, his voice trembling as he tried to reason with his old friend. "Roger… this isn't you. I know you. You're not a killer."

Clyde laughed a sound devoid of humor, hollow and bitter. "Then you don't know me at all, Tom," he replied, his voice breaking slightly, as if confessing an unspoken truth.

A low rumble filled the cave, vibrating through the walls like the slow exhale of a sleeping giant, deep and ominous. Dust and small rocks tumbled from the ceiling, pelting their skin. Caleb, struggling to ignore the searing pain in his shoulder, glanced around at the fragile stone around them, his instincts screaming that they were out of time.

"We don't have time for this!" he shouted, his voice cracking. "The cave's coming down!"

Another rumble shook the ground beneath them, more urgent this time. A jagged crack snaked across the ceiling above, widening by the second. Without another thought, Caleb forced himself to move, lunging forward despite the pain that lanced through his shoulder, grabbing hold of Kate's arm and yanking her out of Clyde's grip.

The sudden movement caught Clyde by surprise. He stumbled backward, his footing slipping as his heel caught on a loose rock. In that heartbeat, Kate reached forward, snatching the detonator from his belt with a fierce determination in her eyes.

"Not today, Clyde," she hissed, clutching the detonator as though it were her own heart.

Before anyone could react, a thunderous crash echoed around them. A massive section of the cave ceiling splintered and fell, rocks and debris raining down in a deadly cascade. Caleb and Kate threw themselves to the side, rolling across the rough stone floor just in time to avoid being crushed.

Clyde wasn't as lucky. His scream was sharp, cut off as a boulder slammed down on his leg, pinning him. Dust hung thick in the air, stinging their eyes and coating their throats, turning every breath into a choke. Clyde's face was twisted with agony, a mix of fury and terror as he fought to free himself.

"Help me!" he screamed, the fury in his eyes mingling with a deep, raw fear. "You can't just leave me here! You owe me!"

Caleb froze, torn between his own simmering anger and the unyielding sense of duty that had driven him through every hardship. His jaw clenched, glancing at Tom, who stared at Clyde with haunted eyes, the weight of years of betrayal heavy in his gaze. Tom took a deep breath, as if he were standing at the edge of a precipice, his expression torn between anger and something deeper—perhaps pity.

With a slow, shuddering exhale, Caleb turned to him. "Help me lift this off him," he said quietly. "If we don't, we're no better than he is."

Tom looked at Caleb, hesitation clear in his eyes, then nodded. Together, they moved to the massive rock, straining against its weight. Every inch was a battle, their bodies aching, muscles burning as they pushed with everything they had. Finally, the stone gave way, freeing Clyde, who slumped forward, his leg twisted at an unnatural angle, his face contorted in pain.

Despite his injury, Clyde's hand inched toward the knife at his side, his fingers trembling but relentless.

"You won't win, Stone," he spat, his voice thick with rage. His face twisted, defiant even now. "This land is already lost. Nothing you do can save it."

Caleb's gaze held Clyde's, steady and unyielding, the anger in his own eyes tempered by something deeper—a fierce determination. He leaned close, his voice so low it was almost a whisper, but each word cut through the noise like a blade.

"Maybe I can't save it all," he said, "but I sure as hell won't let you destroy it."

Another tremor rocked the cave, more intense this time, as if the earth itself was trying to shake them loose. The dust in the air grew thicker, each breath a struggle. Caleb turned to Kate and Tom, urgency burning in his eyes.

"We need to get out. Now!"

Kate grabbed his arm, her fingers digging into his skin. Her face was streaked with dirt and fear, but her eyes held a fierce resolve. "We can't save him if he doesn't want to be saved, Caleb," she said, her voice barely audible.

Tom stood beside them, his face pale, looking at Clyde with the regret of a man who had just lost a lifelong friend. He took a shaky step forward, his voice heavy with sorrow. "Roger, please... for the land, for everything we fought for—don't make this worse."

But Clyde only looked away, his face hardened with resentment. Even with his broken leg, his fingers reached once more for the knife.

Caleb moved without hesitation, stepping forward and delivering a swift, calculated blow. Clyde's head jerked back, and his eyes fluttered before rolling closed, his body sagging as he fell into unconsciousness.

"It's over," Caleb murmured, his voice hollow with exhaustion.

Together, he and Tom dragged Clyde's limp form toward the entrance. Every step was a struggle, the walls around them trembling as though ready to collapse at any moment. The roar of the cave's impending collapse grew louder, a relentless rumble that followed them like an angry beast.

They stumbled out into the storm, the downpour drenching them in an instant. Rain poured down in torrents, mingling with the mud and dirt that covered them. The wind howled, tearing through the trees like a wounded creature. Behind them, the cave let out a final, earth-shaking crash as it caved in completely, burying everything—and everyone—inside.

For a moment, the three of them lay on the wet ground, gasping for air, the storm raging around them, as if the world itself shared in their exhaustion. Caleb's shoulder throbbed, pain radiating down his arm, but he forced himself to sit up, looking over at Kate, who met his gaze with a weary smile.

"What now, Caleb?" she asked, her voice barely carrying over the storm, each word a mix of exhaustion and relief.

He turned, glancing back at the collapsed cave, watching as rain and mud began to fill the jagged cracks. He took a deep breath, his expression a strange combination of weariness and determination.

"We keep fighting," he said finally, his voice quiet but unbreakable. "For the land. For what's left."

Tom knelt beside them, his face etched with regret, the weight of everything that had transpired hanging heavy in his gaze. He looked at Caleb with a new respect, a respect born of shared hardship and the raw truth they had seen in each other.

"I hope you know what you're doing, Stone," Tom murmured, his voice barely a whisper, as though afraid to disturb the fragile peace around them.

Caleb didn't answer immediately. His gaze remained fixed on the horizon, watching as the storm continued to rage, as if it were both an end and a beginning. Finally, he nodded, a faint, resolute smile breaking through his exhaustion.

"So do I, Tom. So do I."

The Quiet Between Trees

The rain had finally stopped, but the air still felt heavy, as if the forest itself hadn't fully exhaled. The early dawn's orange light seeped through the trees, illuminating the drenched ground and casting long, wavering shadows. Caleb Stone stood among the towering pines, his breath clouding the cool air. He was exhausted—body, mind, and spirit. The makeshift bandage on his shoulder was soaked with a mix of rainwater and blood, but he barely felt the physical pain. His exhaustion ran deeper than wounds; it was a weariness that had settled into his bones over years of chasing justice through the tangled paths of Whispering Pines.

Roger Clyde sat a few yards away, bound and battered, his back pressed against a moss-covered boulder. Despite his capture, Clyde's expression was a mix of bitterness and smug defiance. His lips twitched into a half-smile as he eyed Caleb. "You might think you've won," Clyde rasped, his voice rough as if his throat were made of gravel. "But nothing's really changed. You know that, don't you? People here need work, need money. That forest you're so keen on saving is just a pile of lumber waiting to be cut."

The words struck a familiar chord in Caleb—one of doubt, the kind that had haunted him since he'd first taken this job as a park ranger. He'd seen the desperation in the townspeople's eyes, felt the weight of their longing for something better. He knew Clyde wasn't entirely wrong. Jobs were scarce, and Whispering Pines had been on the edge of collapse for years. But that didn't mean the answer was to destroy the very thing that had sustained them for generations.

"The forest is more than that," Caleb said quietly, his voice carrying a calm resolve that belied the turmoil inside him. "It's history, it's culture, it's… survival. It's not just about wood or land; it's about something deeper, something that can't be replaced once it's gone."

Clyde let out a low, cynical laugh. "That's the kind of talk that keeps people poor, Stone. Sentiment doesn't feed families. You'll see—when you're not around to play hero, they'll be back for the trees. It's just a matter of time."

Caleb's eyes hardened. "Maybe. But at least they'll know the truth. And maybe that'll be enough to make some of them think twice."

There was no point in arguing further; Caleb knew that Clyde's beliefs ran as deep as his greed. Turning away, Caleb's gaze shifted to Chief Tom Standing Bear, who sat between two park rangers, his hands cuffed in front of him. Tom's face was pale, lined with regret and the kind of grief that comes from knowing you've betrayed your own people. He caught Caleb's eye, and for a moment, neither spoke. The weight of their shared history lay between them like a fallen tree, immense and immovable.

Tom finally broke the silence, his voice hoarse but steady. "I failed you, Caleb. And I failed my people."

Caleb's throat tightened, emotions tangled in a knot of anger, disappointment, and a strange kind of sympathy. Tom had been a mentor, a guiding force for much of Caleb's adult life. Caleb had looked up to him, trusted him—until the discovery of Tom's involvement in Clyde's scheme. The betrayal had cut deep, but Caleb also understood the complexity of Tom's choices.

"It wasn't just you, Tom," Caleb said after a long pause. "We're all trying to protect something. You were just trying to protect the tribe, even if it meant making deals with the devil."

Tom's eyes filled with a mixture of shame and resignation. "I thought I could find a way to save the tribe by any means necessary. But in the end, I lost sight of what really mattered."

The rangers moved to take Tom away, and as they did, Caleb's mind drifted to his brother. The memories came unbidden, sharp as broken glass. He remembered his brother's laughter, his stubbornness, his passion for the land. His brother had been the first to truly teach him what it meant to love this forest—not as a resource, but as a living, breathing part of their heritage. It was a love that had driven him to his death.

Caleb's chest tightened at the memory. He could still see his brother's face, still hear the excitement in his voice as he'd spoken of plans to protect the park, to ensure that its beauty remained for generations to come. But those dreams had been cut short, replaced by the harsh reality of loss, a reality that Caleb had carried with him ever since.

Kate Jensen's soft footsteps pulled him back to the present. She approached slowly, her face lined with exhaustion but her eyes bright with a fierce determination that had always struck Caleb as both admirable and maddening. She had been there through it all, relentless in her pursuit of the truth. Now, she stood beside him, silent for a moment, her gaze drifting to Tom's departing figure.

"It's a hard thing," Kate said finally, her voice tinged with sadness. "Watching someone like Tom fall."

Caleb nodded, feeling the weight of everything that had happened in the past hours. "He was trying to do the right thing. He just… lost his way."

Kate studied his face, her expression softening. "And what about you, Caleb? What happens now?"

He let out a slow breath, feeling the enormity of the question. "I stay. There's still too much work to be done here. The forest needs someone to stand up for it, even when the odds are against it."

Her gaze lingered on him, a mixture of admiration and something else—something unspoken but felt deeply. "You're a stubborn man, Caleb Stone."

Caleb managed a small, tired smile. "Takes one to know one, Kate Jensen."

For a moment, they simply stood there, side by side, the silence between them filled with the rustling of leaves and the distant call of a bird. It was a silence that held both finality and promise, a moment suspended between what had been and what might still be.

"I have to go," Kate said, her voice breaking the stillness. "There's more work waiting, more places that need protecting. But this place… it's left its mark on me."

He wanted to ask her to stay, to find some way to keep her here, but he knew better. Kate was driven by a purpose that was larger than Whispering Pines, larger than him. "I'll miss you," he said simply.

Her eyes softened, and she stepped closer, pressing a gentle, lingering kiss to his cheek. "I'll miss you too, Caleb. But maybe… someday."

The words hung in the air like an unfinished sentence, filled with potential and regret. As she turned to leave, Caleb felt a pang of loss, sharper than he expected. He watched her walk away, her silhouette disappearing into the mist that still clung to the forest floor. It was a goodbye, but not a permanent one—not if he had anything to say about it.

With Kate gone, Caleb felt the full weight of the forest's silence settle around him. He walked slowly toward the ridge overlooking the valley, his steps heavy but purposeful. The sun was rising now, it's warm, golden light spilling over the treetops, turning the damp leaves into glittering jewels. It was a breathtaking sight, one that stirred something deep within him.

He thought again of his brother, of the dreams they'd shared and the reality they now faced. The forest was scarred—by both human greed and nature's wrath—but it was still here, still standing. Caleb felt a surge of resolve, a promise to himself and to the land. This was his second chance, a chance to honor his brother's memory by fighting for the place they both loved.

He closed his eyes, letting the sounds of the forest wash over him. The whispering leaves, the distant rush of a stream, the faint call of a bird—it was all part of a larger symphony, one that he was determined to protect. It wouldn't be easy. There would be more challenges, more enemies, and more betrayals. But Caleb was ready, more ready than he'd ever been.

The forest had given him a purpose, a sense of redemption that he hadn't believed possible. And as he stood there, his silhouette framed against the vast expanse of Whispering Pines, he felt a quiet certainty settle within him.

Whatever came next, he would face it head-on, for himself, for his brother, and for the silent, enduring beauty of the land that stretched before him.

Where the Trees Remember

The night hung over Whispering Pines, dense and suffocating, shrouded in a silence that seemed to deepen with each passing moment. Caleb Stone stood on the ridge overlooking the forest, where the smuggling ring's final defeat had unfolded in a chaotic surge of events he could still barely process. The tribe's fate teetered on the edge, and though Caleb had been instrumental in unmasking the operation, victory felt hollow. Beneath the triumph lay an ache—a dull, persistent grief that reminded him of the brother he'd lost and the pieces of himself he'd left in these woods.

The forest stretched endlessly before him, each tree a silent witness to the secrets it held. This place had always been more than just trees and soil; it had a soul, an energy that had shaped his life in ways he never imagined. The land had drawn him in, and in many ways, it had offered him solace, purpose. But tonight, it felt like a stranger, its shadows deepened by everything that had happened.

A faint breeze stirred, carrying the scent of wet earth and pine, mingled with the bitter aftertaste of smoke from distant fires that had licked and seared the edges of the park. The air felt thick, weighted with the weight of memory and loss, a tapestry of the past woven into each breath. Caleb inhaled deeply, feeling the pulse of the forest beneath his feet—a steady, ancient rhythm that seemed to mirror his own heartbeat, as though the land itself grieved alongside him. It was a pulse both familiar and alien, like a haunting song that drifted through the trees and into his bones. He exhaled slowly, feeling the weight settle in his chest.

Images of Chief Tom Standing Bear's arrest replayed in his mind, looping like a thread pulled taut and frayed. Tom had been the spirit of the tribe, a pillar of wisdom, a voice that spoke not just for his people but for the land itself, echoing the silent language of the rocks, rivers, and trees. And yet, in the end, he had betrayed them all— whether by necessity or some darker force, Caleb didn't know. There had been no resistance, no anger, not even a glance back as the authorities led him away, his shoulders squared, his face etched with resignation. Caleb could still picture it vividly: the way the chief's eyes had met his, a silent farewell in their depths, a question left unasked and unanswered. For years, Chief Tom had been a mentor, a friend, a guide through the tangled history and legends of this place. Now, those stories seemed hollow, shadows of what they had once been.

Caleb remembered when he first arrived here, an eager park ranger with a head full of ideals, convinced he could bridge the divide between the tribe and the outside world. He'd wanted to help, to protect. Chief Tom had seen that, had taken him under his wing, teaching him to listen, to see beyond what was visible, to understand that some things couldn't be explained by science alone. Caleb had once believed he was building something here, that he could make a difference. Now, as he looked out over the landscape, he wasn't sure if he'd built a bridge or merely deepened the divide.

He blinked, his gaze catching on the faint trace of a footprint in the mud—a reminder of Kate.

His eyes drifted toward the trailhead below, where she had disappeared hours before, leaving a path that only she could walk. She'd stayed with him through the hard moments, her presence a quiet, steady anchor amid the chaos. Caleb had marveled at her resilience, her determination—qualities that reminded him of the forest itself, unyielding and rooted in something larger than any one person. Kate moved through the world with a kind of quiet defiance, a purpose that held her steady even when things crumbled around her. But she, too, had reached a crossroads, her research pulling her away, calling her toward answers that lay beyond this place, beyond him. Though he respected her choice, he couldn't ignore the emptiness she left behind—a hollow space that seemed to echo with everything unspoken.

Caleb thought back to their last conversation, the words that had hovered between them like a fragile promise. They'd walked side by side, their steps slow, a silence falling over them as they approached her car. She'd reached out, her hand brushing against his, her fingers lingering just a moment too long. A gesture simple, yet loaded with meaning, as if that small touch could somehow contain all they could never say. He had wanted to speak, to ask her to stay, but the words had tangled in his throat, caught between loyalty to her dreams and the ache of letting her go.

As she'd driven away, he had stood rooted in place, watching the taillights disappear into the distance. He'd felt hollow then, as though a part of him had left with her. In another life, perhaps, things might have been different. Maybe they would have found a way to bridge the gap between them, to stand together. But they were bound to separate callings, forces that had brought them here and now pulled them apart. He knew it was the right thing, but that knowledge didn't soften the ache that settled deep within him.

Caleb's gaze returned to the expanse of trees stretching before him, each branch and leaf a silent witness to his grief and resilience. The fires had scarred the land, leaving darkened trunks and scorched earth in their wake, yet already the first green shoots were beginning to appear, tiny symbols of life enduring, of rebirth from destruction. He took a step forward, his boots sinking slightly into the damp ground, feeling the forest breathe beneath him. The air was heavy with the promise of rain, a storm gathering somewhere beyond the mountains. Caleb lifted his face to the sky, feeling the brush of wind against his skin, the faint rumble of thunder in the distance.

He didn't know what lay ahead, but he would stay. The land needed him as much as he needed it.

The forest murmured around him, a faint rustling that seemed to rise from the ground itself. Caleb took a step forward, his boots crunching against the damp earth, and he let the sounds of the night envelop him. The weight of his decisions pressed against him, a reminder of everything he'd tried to protect—and everything he'd failed to save.

In his mind, he saw flashes of the past weeks: the mutilated animals, the symbols carved into the trees, the altar deep in the woods where something ancient and dark had stirred. He'd wanted to believe it was just people—desperate, reckless souls trying to make a quick fortune. But the forest had shown him otherwise. There were forces here that defied explanation, forces that neither he nor Kate had fully understood.

Chief Tom had tried to warn him, but Caleb had brushed it off, chalked it up to superstition. Now, standing here in the stillness, he felt the weight of those warnings more than ever. The land held memories—memories of those who had come before, who had honored its spirits, its silent power. Caleb wondered if, in exposing the smuggling ring, he'd inadvertently awakened something that should have remained undisturbed.

The crackling of dry leaves underfoot broke the silence, and Caleb turned, half-expecting to see Kate's familiar figure emerging from the shadows. But there was only the forest, silent and watchful, its darkened branches reaching out like skeletal hands. He exhaled, letting the chill of the night seep into him. This was his home, his sanctuary, and yet tonight, it felt like a place he could never fully know.

He sank down onto a fallen log, letting his gaze drift over the shadowed expanse of trees. The forest was both a refuge and a prison, a place that held both comfort and terror. It was here that he had tried to make peace with his brother's death, to find meaning in the silence that had swallowed him whole. But peace had always been elusive, a fleeting illusion that slipped through his fingers like mist.

He closed his eyes, memories flooding his mind: his brother's laughter, the warmth of his presence, the way they'd explored these woods together, two young men bound by blood and a love for the land. They'd been inseparable, sharing secrets and dreams beneath the canopy of ancient pines. But those days felt distant now, a lifetime away, lost to a world that no longer existed. The forest had been their playground, their sanctuary, and it had betrayed them both.

A chill settled over Caleb's skin, and he opened his eyes, his gaze fixed on the distant horizon where the first traces of dawn were beginning to appear. He'd tried to save his brother, to bring him justice, but in the end, the forest had taken him too. It was a place that demanded sacrifice, a place that held its own rules, its own truths. Caleb had come to accept that, to understand that he couldn't change the past, but he could honor it.

The sound of footsteps caught his attention, and he turned to see Chief Tom approaching, his figure blending into the shadows like a ghost. The man's face was etched with weariness, his shoulders heavy with the weight of the tribe's uncertain future. Caleb rose, meeting the chief's gaze, and for a moment, they stood in silence, two men bound by a shared history and a fractured trust.

"Caleb," Tom's voice was low, carrying a sadness Caleb hadn't heard before. It was a deep, mournful tone, as though he were not just speaking to Caleb but confessing to the very earth beneath their feet. "You did what you had to do. But the land... it won't forget."

Caleb nodded, feeling the truth of those words settle into him like the roots of the towering trees around them. The land held its own memory, its own history, one that would continue long after they were gone. For as long as he could remember, this forest had been his refuge, his teacher. It had a way of absorbing human sorrow, softening the wounds people left behind. But this time felt different—like a scar left on the land itself. He met Tom's gaze, and in that instant, he didn't see a fallen leader, nor the traitor who had betrayed his people, but a man whose choices had led him down a path from which he couldn't return.

"I don't regret stopping you, Tom." Caleb's voice was steady, though a slight tremor ran beneath it. "But I wish... I wish things could have been different. I wish you hadn't made it so that I had to choose."

Tom's gaze softened. The lines etched in his face, worn by years of struggle and sacrifice, deepened as he looked at Caleb, his expression a strange mix of remorse and resignation. He placed a hand on Caleb's shoulder, his grip firm yet gentle. "So do I. But we are bound to this place, Caleb. It's in our blood, our bones. It shapes us, whether we like it or not. Even when it feels like it's against us."

They stood together in silence, the weight of their choices settling heavily between them, as if the air itself had thickened with the burden. Caleb could hear the rustling of leaves, the faint call of a bird in the distance, the quiet murmur of the forest waking up. It reminded him of the first time he'd stepped into these woods as a child, wide-eyed and ready to discover all its hidden wonders. Back then, he'd believed the forest would always be a place of peace, a constant in a world of change. But that belief had fractured like fragile glass, leaving him holding shards of truth that cut deeper than he'd ever expected.

He turned his gaze to the horizon, where the first rays of sunlight began to break, casting a golden glow over the treetops. The light filtered through the branches, illuminating the forest in a gentle hue that seemed to soften even the harshest shadows. Caleb watched as the trees welcomed the morning, their leaves catching the light, shimmering with a brilliance that felt almost sacred. It was as though the forest itself was acknowledging what they had lost and what they had gained.

A part of him wanted to ask Tom one last question, to understand what had led him to the decisions he had made. But he already knew the answer. Tom's actions hadn't been born out of malice but of desperation—a desperate attempt to protect what he loved, even if it meant crossing lines he'd once vowed never to cross. Caleb could see that now, in the way Tom's shoulders slumped, the weight of his choices pressing down on him.

"You'll go back to them?" Caleb asked quietly, the words more of a statement than a question.

Tom nodded. "Yes. They deserve to know the truth. And they deserve a leader who won't betray them."

The acceptance in Tom's voice surprised Caleb. There was no defensiveness, no attempt to justify his actions. Just the quiet resignation of a man who had made his peace with his fate. And as Tom turned to leave, Caleb felt a sense of closure he hadn't expected—a quiet acceptance of the path they had both chosen, each one bearing the weight of their choices alone.

The light shifted, casting elongated shadows across the forest floor, a silent reminder of the presence of those who had come before, of lives lived and lost in these woods. Caleb watched as Tom's figure receded into the trees, his silhouette swallowed by the shifting light and shadow. The chief would return to his people, to the life he had known. But Caleb would stay. He would remain here, a silent guardian of a place that held both beauty and darkness.

Taking a deep breath, Caleb let the cool morning air fill his lungs, savoring the earthy scent of the forest floor mixed with the crispness of dawn. This was his home, his sanctuary, a place that had shaped him as much as he had shaped it. The forest had seen his greatest joys, his deepest sorrows, and now it bore witness to his decision to stay—to protect what remained, to safeguard the secrets buried within its depths.

The wind stirred through the branches, whispering a soft, haunting melody that seemed to carry the voices of those who had walked these trails before him, those who had loved and fought for this land just as he did. He closed his eyes, letting the sound wash over him, feeling a deep sense of belonging, of purpose. He was exactly where he was meant to be.

A small bird chirped nearby, its song piercing the quiet. Caleb opened his eyes, watching as it flitted from branch to branch, its movements light and unburdened. He felt a pang of envy, wishing he could shake off the weight of his choices so easily. But he knew that wasn't his path. His path lay here, among the trees, in the quiet shadows and dappled sunlight, in the timeless rhythm of the forest.

And he knew, as he stood there with the morning light washing over him, that he would endure. The forest would endure. And together, they would weather whatever came next, standing as silent witnesses to the world's changes and its scars.

Caleb's hand brushed the rough bark of the nearest tree, feeling the solid strength beneath his fingertips. He took a final deep breath, letting the morning air settle into him, grounding him. Whatever the future held, he was ready to face it head-on.